**'I was deva...
admitted.**

'I told myself how ... had only been one night, after all, but it was so hard to put it into perspective.'

Jack nodded. 'I felt the same. I couldn't forget. I thought I'd got past it, but then I saw you again and it all came back as though it was yesterday. And then I learned you had a daughter, and I assumed you had found someone else and got married.'

'Assumptions,' Hannah murmured. 'Dangerous things.'

'I wasn't completely wrong, though, was I? There was someone else.'

'There was only Olivia's father,' Hannah said.

Jack held her gaze and Hannah was engulfed by his compassion. Had he forgiven her for not telling him about Olivia?

'Do you want me to tell you who Olivia's father is?'

'No,' he said very softly. 'I don't think you need to tell me that, do you?'

Alison Roberts lives in Christchurch, New Zealand. She began her working career as a primary school teacher, but now juggles available working hours between writing and active duty as an ambulance officer. Throwing in a large dose of parenting, housework, gardening and pet-minding keeps life busy, and teenage daughter Becky is responsible for an increasing number of days spent on equestrian pursuits. Finding time for everything can be a challenge, but the rewards make the effort more than worthwhile.

Recent titles by the same author:

A COURAGEOUS DOCTOR
CONSULTANT IN CRISIS
   (City Search and Rescue Book 1)
THE NURSE'S RESCUE
   (City Search and Rescue Book 2)
DOCTOR AT RISK
   (City Search and Rescue Book 3)
THE SURGEON'S CHILD

THE DOCTOR'S SECRET FAMILY

BY
ALISON ROBERTS

*First published in Great Britain 2004
Harlequin Mills & Boon Limited,
Eton House, 18-24 Paradise Road, Richmond, Surrey TW9 1SR*

© Alison Roberts 2004

ISBN 0 263 83914 1

*Set in Times Roman 10½ on 12 pt.
03-0804-48921*

*Printed and bound in Spain
by Litografía Rosés, S.A., Barcelona*

CHAPTER ONE

IT JUST wouldn't go away.

The nasty prickle of premonition had been stalking senior paediatric registrar Hannah Campbell ever since she had first woken that morning, and she had been unable to shake it off despite a busy few hours on ward duty. At least now Hannah thought she had identified its origin.

'I have a horrible feeling I'm not going to get it.'

'Of course you will.' Junior registrar William Price sounded surprised. 'I wish I had a fraction of your skill in getting IV access in kids.'

Hannah glanced up from the tiny hand she was holding, bent over to stretch the skin between wrist and knuckles in the hope of revealing the exact whereabouts of a vein. 'I'm not talking about IV access, Will. I'm talking about the job.'

'Ah…' William rearranged his hold on the infant lying on the treatment bed. 'It's OK, Jamie,' he said soothingly. 'It'll all be over in a minute or two.' He turned his gaze back to his senior colleague. 'They've closed the applications for the consultancy position now, haven't they?'

'Yeah.' Hannah was using an alcohol wipe in a circular motion to clean Jamie's hand and hopefully stimulate a tiny vein into making an appearance. 'They closed yesterday.' Which had to be why this feeling of premonition had started first thing this morning. The countdown to the interviews was on.

'Do you know how many applicants there were?'

'Not exactly. But I do know that one of them is from a guy in Auckland who is already a consultant and has years more experience than me. He wants to get out of the rat race up there and move his family to Christchurch.'

'You have the advantage of being known. How long have you worked here now?'

'I was a junior registrar here nearly six years ago. I had a year off before I got the senior registrar position. That was three and a half years ago now.'

'You had the year off because of Olivia?'

'Mmm.' Hannah had selected the finest gauge of cannula available. 'Sorry about this, sweetie,' she murmured as she pierced the skin on Jamie's hand.

The eleven-month-old boy's grizzles increased in volume and William had to hold his arm more firmly to prevent any movement. The child's mother had elected not to watch the procedure so the two young doctors were alone in the treatment room of Christchurch Central Hospital's paediatric ward.

'I wouldn't worry about it.' William's reassuring tone was intended to benefit the baby as much as Hannah. 'Peter thinks you're marvellous and as head of department he'll have significant input into deciding who gets the job.'

'I hope so.' The worry wasn't going to evaporate easily, however. Hannah wanted this position she had waited a long time to apply for. She wanted it badly.

She also wanted to find IV access in this severely dehydrated infant. IV fluid resuscitation was urgent and she wasn't going to allow any niggling personal fears to interfere with her performance. She should also be using this opportunity to help consolidate William's skills, not discuss her future employment options.

'What percentage dehydration would you estimate Jamie to have?' Hannah was advancing the fine needle in a new direction now. Anatomically, there had to be a vein somewhere close.

'His skin's a bit mottled and the capillary return isn't great,' William answered promptly. 'His fontanelle and eyes are markedly sunken but his level of consciousness isn't too depressed. I'd say about seven per cent.'

Hannah nodded. She drew the needle back towards the surface of the skin and a tiny spot of red appeared in the flashback chamber of the cannula mechanism.

'Got you,' she said in satisfaction. 'Keep him really still for a second, Will.' Dropping the angle of the needle and advancing it just fractionally, Hannah held her breath as she pushed the plastic cannula off the end of the needle. A smooth entry indicated effective placement and Hannah unsnapped the tourniquet fastening before swiftly removing the introducing needle and attaching a syringe to the end of the cannula.

'What tests are you going to order on these bloods, Will?'

'CBC and differential. Urea, creatinine, sodium and potassium levels.'

'What's the most likely cause for the gastroenteritis?'

'Rotavirus.'

'And how are we going to treat it?'

'Initial fluid resuscitation with normal saline at 20 mil per kilogram. Then 10 mil per kilogram per hour until we get the serum electrolyte results. We'll adjust the solution depending on sodium levels after that.'

'Cool.' Hannah attached the giving set leading to the bag of IV fluid already set up on the drip stand. She taped the line to Jamie's arm and then protected the IV cannulation site with a thick layer of crêpe bandaging. When finally satisfied that the fluids were running well, Hannah relaxed and scooped the baby from the table into her arms.

'There you go, darling,' she murmured. 'All done. Let's get you back to Mummy for a cuddle.'

William grinned. 'You must be one heck of a substitute. That's the closest to being happy I've seen him look since he arrived. What is it with you and babies?'

Hannah kissed the top of the downy head. 'I'm just the maternal type, I guess. There's got to be some reward for the awful things we need to do to the poor wee mites sometimes.'

'Mind you don't take a dose of rotavirus home to Olivia.'

'I've been taking things home since she was even younger than Jamie. I reckon we've both got fantastic immune systems by now. Livvy never gets sick.'

Hannah's pager sounded as they walked back to Jamie's room. 'I'll leave you to get those bloods away and chase up the results, Will. Keep a close eye on things. If Jamie's condition deteriorates any further, we'll need to transfer him to Intensive Care.'

There was a phone on the wall just outside the room Jamie would share with his mother for the next day or two. William emerged just as Hannah finished taking the call her pager message had requested.

'You don't look very happy,' he commented. 'What's up?'

'I have to get up to Theatre. A woman who's thirty-five weeks pregnant has just come in with a placental separation following an MVA. They're rushing her up for an emergency Caesar and it seems I'm the most senior paediatrician available at the moment.' Hannah was already moving swiftly towards the lifts at the end of the wide corridor. Maybe the cause of that premonition had been some instinct that she might be faced with a particularly challenging case. Thanks to Hannah's determination to excel in everything she did in the run-up to the decision on appointing the department's new consultant she had a new pressure and a whole new set of nerves to contend with.

'You'll be fine.' William's confident words floated through the closing lift doors. 'Peter will be proud of you, you'll see.'

Consultant Peter Smiley was living up to his name when he sat down at the table in the cafeteria Hannah was occupying nearly two hours later. It was far too late to be considered part of any normal lunch-break and the huge room was largely deserted.

'I've been hearing great things about you, Dr Campbell.'

Hannah grinned. If that emergency case had been responsible for the nameless fear stalking her earlier then she had managed to prove her instinct very wrong. Her grin faded as she shook her head.

'I have to admit I was pretty nervous when I got to Theatre. I had no idea how long the baby might have been hypoxic for. I had the feeling that even if the resuscitation was successful the parents might not thank me for it.' Hannah bit her lip. 'What *are* the precise criteria for deciding not to take an aggressive approach? Have you ever done a resus and left parents to cope with bringing up a badly handicapped child, Pete?'

'It happens.' Peter nodded. 'But there are no hard and fast rules. Even when you get a baby born at the limits of viability, like twenty-two to twenty-four weeks' gestation, it's tricky. You have to look at the weight and degree of bruising, along with the baby's condition at birth, the presence or absence of a heartbeat and any efforts to breathe.'

Hannah nodded. 'This one had an Apgar score of zero initially. White, flaccid, undetectable heartbeat and no spontaneous breathing.'

'What gestation?'

'Thirty-five weeks.'

'How badly injured was the mother?'

'She had a fractured tib-fib and seat-belt bruising. It was probably the position of the seat belt that caused the placental separation. She'd begun bleeding heavily by the time she reached the emergency department. They did a quick ultrasound and got her straight up to Theatre. The baby was delivered within thirty minutes of her arrival, which was pretty amazing.'

'I'll say. They must have had a theatre ready to go.'

'They were setting up an elective Caesar. The patient had had her epidural and was on the way. I bet she wasn't too happy about being sent back to the ward for another couple of hours.'

'No.' Peter sat back in his chair, his gaze curious. 'So, what did you do with this flaccid baby?'

'Put her under the lights and used gentle suction to clear the upper airway. Inflating her lungs with the bag mask initiated a gasp but no spontaneous breathing so I intubated.'

Peter raised his eyebrows. Intubation of a newborn required considerable skill. Clumsy insertion of the tube could damage the upper airways, and over-vigorous inflation could damage the lungs. 'Any problems?'

'No. I ventilated at a rate of thirty per minute with a

nice gentle pressure but she still didn't pink up. Heart rate was less than sixty per minute so then I started cardiac massage.' Hannah's smile was a little grim. She had thought she was fighting a losing battle at that point. She had encircled the baby's chest with both hands, positioning her thumbs to exert pressure on the lower half of the tiny sternum and directing the nurse assisting her to deliver one inflation of the lungs to every three to five compressions.

'Did you need any adrenaline?'

'I had it drawn up as I cannulated the umbilical vein but then things started to improve.' Hannah's smile was much brighter now. 'The Apgar score at five minutes was 7. She had facial grimaces, gasping respiration, heart rate greater than a hundred, some flexion and she was finally pink!'

Peter smiled at Hannah's obvious pleasure. 'Pretty satisfying, then?'

'You bet. Apgar was 9 at ten minutes. I still wasn't happy enough with her muscle tone to give her a ten but I'm pretty confident she'll be OK. It's hard to know, though, isn't it?' Hannah's brow furrowed. 'She could have been without oxygen for long enough to have permanent repercussions.'

'Some people put all sorts of things down to a mild hypoxic insult—anything from hyperactivity to learning problems. But there's not much in the way of good evidence. Babies can recover remarkably well from what seems like a dire start to life. We'll keep an eye on this one for the next few days for any sign of neurological compromise but I doubt we'll find anything. You sound like you managed a difficult case extremely well, Hannah. Well done.' The consultant's face creased into a familiar expression of approval. 'I'm proud of you.'

'Thanks.' Hannah returned the fond smile. 'If I'm good at what I do a lot of credit needs to go to you, you know.'

'It's always been a pleasure to work with you, Hannah. A pleasure that I hope will continue for a long time.'

'So do I.' Hannah toyed with her almost empty cup of coffee. 'I'm going to be biting my nails waiting for this consultancy to be decided.'

'You really want this job, don't you?'

'It's exactly what I want, Pete.'

'But it's only a seven-tenths position and you don't want to do any private practice, do you?'

'Will that make a difference?' Hannah asked anxiously. 'Do you really need someone else in your practice?'

'I will eventually. I'm not getting any younger, in case you hadn't noticed.'

Peter was nearly sixty years old but Hannah grinned. 'I hadn't. You'll need to develop some more crinkles, as Livvy calls them.'

'I've got plenty of "crinkles".' Peter's face brightened. 'How is Livvy?'

'She's great. She can write her own name now. She drew the most amazing picture yesterday and signed it for me. I think I'll get it framed.'

'What's it a picture of?'

'Joseph.'

'That's your...donkey, yes?''

Hannah laughed. 'That's the one.'

'It's a bit difficult remembering all the names of your pets. Every one of those hens has a name, doesn't it?'

'Yes. And the goat and cats. We'd love to get a puppy some time as well.'

'How on earth do you look after them all?'

'It's not difficult. And if I get this consultancy I'll have a bit more time at home so maybe we could think about getting a dog.'

'Is that why you're so keen?'

'Of course not. Having more time with Livvy is the main appeal. On a consultant's salary I would be paid as much for seven-tenths as I am for this registrar position, which feels like twelve-tenths a lot of the time. Plus I'd be able to stay in Christchurch on a permanent basis. Neither Livvy nor I want to leave our property. I've spent years turning that old house into something worth living in and I'd hate to move. We'd never find land so close to town that we could afford now either. The prices for lifestyle blocks have gone through the roof in the last few years.'

'So the department doesn't really rate, then?'

'Come off it, Pete.' Hannah's admonishing tone was negated by the smile she bestowed on her boss. 'You've been far more than a boss, or even a colleague, to me and you know it. I might never have come back after having Livvy if it hadn't been for your encouragement, and thanks to you, the paediatric department of Christchurch Central is probably more sought after as a place to work in than anywhere else in this country.' She sighed. 'That's the problem. I'm going to be up against some pretty stiff competition for this position, aren't I?'

'I wouldn't worry too much about that. I was just discussing you with Tom Berry, in fact.'

'Oh?' Tom Berry was one of the paediatric surgeons at Central. He would also be on the committee that would decide the position. Hannah widened her eyes anxiously but Peter simply grinned.

'He had very nice things to say about you.' Peter

glanced at his watch. 'And that reminds me. I was supposed to be in Tom's office ten minutes ago for an afternoon tea to welcome *their* new appointee.' He stood up hurriedly. 'I'll have to disappear. Sorry, Hannah.'

'That's OK.' Hannah followed his example and rose, collecting her empty plate and cup. 'I'm due back in the ward for an admission anyway.'

Her resigned expression made Peter smile. 'Anyone I know?'

'Jadine Milton,' Hannah replied. 'She looks set to become our latest frequent flyer.'

'Abdominal pain again?'

'Yep. And I've ruled out every obscure medical cause I can think of over the last three admissions.'

'Crohn's disease? Constipation? Lead poisoning?' Peter was walking with Hannah as she left the cafeteria.

'And intussusception, intestinal obstruction, appendicitis, pyelonephritis and pancreatitis.'

'Diabetes?'

'Blood sugars are normal. I'm sure there's no organic cause. We even did an endoscopy last time to rule out peptic ulcers.'

'Munchausen's?'

'It's starting to look like that. Or Munchausen's by proxy. The mother's got a few problems.'

'Who initiated today's admission?'

'The GP. I suspect she's fed up.'

Peter turned off as they reached the lifts near the gift shop in the main foyer. 'Get some input from Psych this time. And maybe Social Services.'

Hannah nodded wearily. 'I'll see if I can have a good talk to the mother myself as well.' She headed for the stairs unsurprised that that vague feeling of premonition had returned. This was another challenging case but behavioural and social problems were veering away from any field of expertise Hannah had and it was hard to stay uninvolved when she liked her patient. Six-year-old Jadine was not unlike her own daughter to look at, with her blond curls and big, brown eyes. Her single mother was also struggling with the kinds of issues Hannah had dealt with herself. The case would be time-consuming, however, and there were a lot of loose ends on the ward that Hannah would need to deal with before she could leave for the day. She almost welcomed that familiar tension that came with the conflict between wanting to get home to Livvy and needing to do her job as best she could. She was used to coping with this and it was preferable to that formless fear still clouding her day.

Jadine Milton lay on a bed in Room 4, next door to where young Jamie was receiving IV fluids to correct his dehydration. The small girl's face was pale but Hannah suspected this was quite a normal colour for her. Clutching a Barbie doll, Jadine was shaking her head vigorously as Hannah entered the room.

'I don't want a drink, Mummy. I *hate* water!'

'Water's good for you. You drink far too much cola. It's probably got something to do with all these tummyaches you're getting.'

'Hi, there, pumpkin.' Hannah smiled at her patient. 'Fancy seeing you in here again.'

'I'm so sorry about this.' Jadine's mother, Caroline Briggs, sighed theatrically. 'I felt embarrassed enough turning up at the medical centre yet again. It's even worse to have to come back into hospital. I know how busy you are and—'

'It's not a problem,' Hannah interrupted. 'What's important is making sure that Jadine is fine.'

'You haven't found anything wrong with her the last three times she's been in. You must be starting to think we just make a fuss about nothing.'

Hannah hoped her smile was reassuring. She could see the anxiety in Jadine's face. No matter what the cause of the recurrent abdominal pain, a six-year-old child couldn't be held responsible for any wastage of time and resources.

'So your tummy's sore again, Jadine?'

The little girl nodded.

'Does it feel just the same as last time?'

She nodded again.

'When did it start?'

'It's never really gone away completely,' her mother answered. 'She seems to get better and then it comes back again a few days later. It's been going on for weeks.'

Hannah nodded. The first admission had been six weeks ago now. 'Is there any pattern to it?'

'How do you mean?'

'Is it more likely to happen, say, on a Monday? Or a weekend?'

'I don't know. She's been missing an awful lot of school, though.'

'Do you like school, Jadine?'

Jadine nodded again. 'My friend Georgie and me play Barbies at lunchtime.'

It was not the kind of response she would have expected from a child who might be experiencing problems like bullying at school. Hannah glanced up at Caroline.

'Have you noticed anything that seems to make any difference?'

'Like what?'

'Changes in her diet, maybe?'

'The only real change she gets is when she goes to stay with my mum.' Caroline sighed. 'For some reason she'll always eat her veggies when she's staying with Grandma. She never does it at home.'

'Don't you like veggies, Jadine?'

'I like Grandma's veggies.'

'I cook them exactly the same way,' Caroline protested.

'They don't taste the same. And you don't make pudding. I have to eat veggies for Gran or I don't get the pudding.'

'I don't have time to make puddings. And, anyway, they're not good for you.'

'Gran's puddings are good for me. They make my tummy stop being sore.'

Hannah stayed silent, observing the undercurrent between mother and daughter. The significance of another family member being involved was not something she had thought of pursuing in this case but there was clearly something going on here that could be important. She made a mental note to follow it up.

'Have you been back to your GP before today?'

'We've been at the medical centre every other day. They're getting sick of seeing us turn up and it's costing me a fortune.'

Hannah smiled sympathetically. The referral note from the GP had suggested that Jadine's mother needed more reassurance than they were able to supply. 'Is she eating all right?'

'She'll eat anything that looks like a hamburger or chips. Her appetite seems to vanish in front of a plate of vegetables, though.' Caroline sighed again. 'I *do* try.'

Hannah smiled as she sat on the edge of the bed close to Jadine. 'My little girl likes chips, too.' She leaned forward. 'She's got a Barbie doll as well, only she left hers in the water trough out in our paddock the other day and now Barbie keeps leaking.'

Jadine stared at Hannah. 'What's a troff?'

'A big drinking bowl. Like cows or horses need.'

'Have you got a cow?'

'No. I haven't got a horse either, but I do have a donkey.'

'What's its name?'

'Joseph.'

Caroline was also staring at Hannah. 'Why do you have a donkey?'

Hannah laughed. 'Just for a pet. I'd always wanted one.'

'Why?'

'They're lovely animals. Very gentle and friendly and they're kind of peaceful to be around.'

'Really?' Caroline still looked unconvinced. 'I thought they made a horrible noise.'

'Joseph is very quiet. Except for when he sees us coming and wants to say hello.' Hannah pulled her stethoscope from its position around her neck. Chatting with her patient might make for a relaxing atmosphere but it was time she got on with her job.

'Can I have a look at you now, Jadine? I need to check all those things like your blood pressure and temperature and heart and then I'll need to feel your tummy.'

Jadine's eyes filled with tears. 'Do I have to have a needle again?'

Her mother grabbed a tissue from the box on the locker and was ready to mop her daughter's face. 'You've got to be brave, Jadie. Dr Hannah's here to make you better.'

'You don't have to have a blood test right now,' Hannah said soothingly. 'And if you need one later we'll make sure we put that special cream on your skin to make it go all numb so it doesn't hurt.'

Hannah went through the motions of a full physical examination. Consciously trying not to allow any bias towards a psychosomatic cause for the abdominal pain probably made her examination even more thorough than normal. As the commonest acute surgical emergency of childhood and usually seen in children over five years of age, appendicitis was still at the forefront of possible diagnoses but, as with the previous three admissions, there was no associated low-grade fever and no history of vomiting or anorexia. Whilst Jadine seemed to have genuine discomfort on palpation, Hannah could find no 'guarding', where the muscles became protectively rigid, when she pressed on the lower right quadrant of the abdomen.

'Bowel habits normal?' she queried.

'Absolutely.' Jadine's mother nodded. 'Colour and everything's just the same as usual. I always check.'

Hannah hid her surprise. She might not have blinked if an infant's mother knew more about her baby's bowel habits than her own but it was a little unusual for a six-year-old not to be demanding some privacy in the toilet. Her own daughter was four and a half now. She might not bother to shut the door and she sometimes forgot to flush but she had been independent as far as toileting went for some time now.

'Has Jadine had any bugs recently? Coughs or colds?' An upper respiratory tract infection could cause inflammation of the mesenteric lymph nodes leading to nonspecific abdominal pain but Jadine's lungs sounded as clear as bells, which fitted with Caroline's denial of any viral illnesses.

'You don't have a family history of migraine, do you, Caroline?'

'You asked me that last time. I get headaches.' Caroline's huff was resigned. 'Usually when the bills are due to be paid. Wouldn't call them migraines, though.'

Hannah nodded. Children who went on to have classical migraines commonly presented with recurrent episodes of prolonged abdominal pain but they usually had nausea or other symptoms accompanying the discomfort. As Caroline had pointed out, she was covering the same ground she had been over before.

'We'll need to get a urine sample again.' She smiled at Jadine. 'Do you remember that test, sweetie? The nurse takes you to the toilet and gives you a wash and you have to wee into the little jar. You don't mind doing that again for us, do you?'

Jadine shook her head.

'Good girl. That way we can do another check to make sure there's no bugs hiding in your waterworks that might be making your tummy sore.' And it might give Hannah a chance to have a talk to Jadine's mother privately. 'You tell me when you think you might be ready to go to the toilet.'

'I want to go now.'

'Do you? That's great.' Hannah stood up. 'I'll call Nina to come and look after you. She's your nurse today, isn't she?'

Jadine smiled. 'Nina's nice. She likes Barbies.'

'She looks a bit like Barbie, doesn't she, with that pretty blond hair?' Hannah smiled. 'It's just like yours, isn't it?'

Jadine returned the smile happily, which only reinforced Hannah's impression that there was nothing seriously wrong with this child. 'I'm going to take Mum off for a cup of tea while Nina's looking after you,' she told Jadine. 'Is that OK?'

'Sounds good to me,' Caroline said. 'I'd love a cup of tea.' She eyed the notes Hannah was carrying anxiously, however, as the two women took their tea into Hannah's office a few minutes later. 'You've found something wrong with her, haven't you? Something you didn't want to talk about in front of Jadie.'

'Not at all,' Hannah said promptly. 'It was time I had a break and I'm sure you could use one. It's pretty stressful having your child unwell.'

Caroline sat down on the spare chair in the office. 'How old is your daughter?'

'Four and a half.'

'Ah…nice age.' Caroline's smile was poignant. 'Make the most of it.' She caught Hannah's glance. 'It won't be long till she starts school,' she added. 'And that's when you really lose your baby.'

'It's a big milestone,' Hannah agreed. 'But we're both looking forward to it.'

'Are you?' Caroline sounded surprised. 'I cried for days. It wasn't until I started being a mother help at school every day that things started to get better.'

'Oh?' The sound was intended to be encouraging but a warning bell was going off for Hannah. Just how deeply centred on her child was Caroline Briggs's life? Munchausen syndrome by proxy was an unusual and bizarre form of child abuse that could possibly be triggered by a parent's need for some form of attention. Was Jadine Caroline's primary source of relationships with others?

Given Caroline's concern about a prolonged and unexplained illness in her child, the syndrome needed consideration. And hadn't Jadine said her symptoms disappeared when she stayed with her grandmother? It was highly unlikely that she was being cured by some magic ingredients in the puddings. Hannah would need to seek assistance from other medical professionals, as Peter had suggested. A conversation with the grandmother was probably overdue as well but now seemed like a good opportunity to gather some more background history.

'Tell me about Jadine when she was a baby,' Hannah invited. 'Did everything go well with your pregnancy and her birth?'

'Depends what you mean by "well",' Caroline said heavily. 'Getting pregnant was an accident, you know. I was only eighteen.'

Hannah nodded sympathetically. She had been twenty-eight and old enough to have known better, but she had learned the hard way about accidental pregnancies herself.

'Dave, my boyfriend, wanted me to have an abortion but it was too late by then and, anyway, I didn't want one.'

Hannah nodded again. It was an issue that had to be confronted by virtually every woman with an unplanned pregnancy but it had never rated more than a dismissive thought from herself. Maybe it had been easier being the only person involved in the decision-making process.

'And I really wanted to marry Dave. I thought the baby would keep us together.'

Maybe the pregnancy hadn't been so accidental in Caroline's case. Hannah couldn't imagine wanting to marry the father of her child. In the weeks before she had discovered she was pregnant, she had been more than happy with the thought that she would never have to see or speak to him again.

'I never did well at school,' Caroline continued.

'Dropped out when I was fifteen. I knew I could be a good mum, though. It was all I ever really wanted to be.'

Hannah was silent. If feelings of self-worth came only from motherhood then a child starting school and beginning to move towards independence could present a problem. Not one that Hannah had ever had to face, however. She had worked hard at school and done exceptionally well. Her dream of going to medical school and becoming a doctor had been too much a part of her to be anything but temporarily superseded by becoming a parent. Not that Livvy wasn't just as important in her life as her career but they represented totally different parts of who she was. And it didn't make her a bad mother. Hannah knew she did both her 'jobs' well.

'It worked for a while,' Caroline sighed, 'but he walked out on us when Jadie was two.'

'That must have been tough.'

'Yeah.' The tone was bitter. 'If it hadn't been for my mum, I wouldn't have survived.'

'You were lucky to have her, then.' Hannah had had no family to help her. She had had to cope on her own. Emotionally, financially, physically. It hadn't been easy but it had made her strong and in retrospect Hannah was glad it had been that way. She could handle whatever life chose to throw at her now, which why the odd feeling that there was something looming to be afraid of was so disconcerting. She had been through so much—what could happen that would be worse?

She tuned out the sound of Caroline's voice listing the various crises with unpaid bills and the usual medical woes involved in raising a child as the horrible thought struck. Had she been tempting fate telling William about her daughter's fantastic immune system? Or boasting that she never got sick? Livvy could get sick. *Really* sick. That would be the worst thing that could happen. A need to see her child and reassure herself followed hot on the heels of acknowledging that fear, and Hannah stole a glance at her watch. At this rate it might be hours before she could leave to collect her daughter.

'I did most of it by myself.' Caroline sounded defensive now. 'I'm a good mother. I never put Jadie in child care. I did everything for her. I still do.'

Hannah simply nodded again. She wasn't going to allow her own guilt buttons regarding child care to be pushed. She'd never been lucky enough to have a choice. Not with the kind of debt that medical training had left her with. She focused on Caroline as she finished her cup of tea. There were enough clues to make Hannah believe that a psychiatric evaluation of Jadine's family circumstances would be worthwhile.

'Jadine should be back in her room by now.' Hannah stood up to signal an end to the conversation. 'Will you be staying in with her tonight?'

'I can't.'

Hannah couldn't help looking surprised. During the previous three admissions, it had been an uphill battle to persuade Caroline to even take an extended break from being with her daughter.

'I've got a…date,' Caroline confessed as she followed Hannah from the office. 'He lives in Wellington and doesn't get down this way very often. I'll be back first thing in the morning, though.'

'That's fine,' Hannah said calmly. 'We'll take good care of Jadine.'

She tucked the additional snippet of information away. So Caroline's attention was being diverted to some extent away from her daughter. Munchausen's was still a possibility but maybe it wasn't by proxy. Perhaps Jadine was trying to find a way of dealing with the competition or a perceived rejection by her mother. Hannah's query as the two women neared Room 4 was deliberately casual.

'Does Jadine's father still see her at all?'

'*No.*' The response was vehement. 'And I intend to keep it that way, thanks.'

Hannah was quite grateful for an interruption from William, which precluded digging any further into the new can of worms she had opened regarding Jadine Milton's family problems. He waited until Caroline had gone through the door of Room 4.

'I've got Jamie's serum electrolyte results. Sodium's well above 150 mmol per litre so he's hypernatraemic.'

'Have you adjusted the IV solution?'

'I've started 0.2 normal saline in 4.3 per cent glucose.'

'Plus KCl?'

William nodded. 'Thirty to 40 mmol per litre.'

'Good. Restrict fluid to 150 mmol per kilo for the first twenty-four hours. We need to aim for total correction over about forty-eight hours. How's he looking?'

'A lot better.'

'That's good.' Hannah was eyeing her open office door and thinking of the phone on her desk. A quick call to the Maysfield Child Care Centre to set her own mind at rest would make her feel a lot better. 'Anything else going on that I should know about?'

'No. Things are pretty quiet generally. About time you headed home, isn't it?'

'I won't argue with that.' It was only 4 p.m. but Hannah always started at 7.30 a.m. so she could leave before 5 when she wasn't on call and get a few hours with Livvy before bedtime. She could take her paperwork

home with her. It might take a while to find an appropriate way to document her suspicions about Jadine
Milton, and a quiet hour late this evening would be a lot
easier than trying to do it here, with the inevitable in-
terruptions that would occur.

It would also mean she didn't have to appear over-
anxious by ringing the child care centre with no reason
other than to enquire whether her daughter looked
healthy. She would find out soon enough for herself.
Prompted by her desire to get away, Hannah hurriedly
bundled up the paperwork she needed from her desk,
stuffing it into her briefcase as she headed briskly for
the door. She hadn't quite secured her armload as she
entered the corridor and turned to pull her door shut. Her
movements were still swift. Far too swift to prevent a
near collision as she swung around again to move towards the exit.

'Whoops!' Peter Smiley's tone commiserated for the
fact that Hannah's paperwork was now strewn all over
the floor but Hannah couldn't have cared less about the
mishap. She hadn't even seen the shower of paper. She
was too stunned to move her gaze away from the man
standing beside Peter.

'I was just coming to find you,' Peter said cheerfully.
'We're doing the tour.' Anything odd about Hannah's
expression was apparently being dismissed as embarrassment due to a clumsy moment. 'This is our new consultant surgeon for Paediatrics, Hannah…Jack Douglas.'

Suddenly Hannah knew that her premonition had had
nothing to do with her job application. Or any challenging case. Or her daughter's state of health.

She had been right to trust her instincts because the
premonition of disaster had been spot on.

The disaster was standing right in front of her. As

large as life. And its mouth was moving. A rich, deep rumble of words sent reinforcements to enhance the paralysing visual effects Hannah was still experiencing.

'Hello, Hannah,' Jack Douglas said. 'This is a bit of a surprise, isn't it?'

CHAPTER TWO

IT WASN'T a surprise.

A surprise, in Hannah's book, carried the connotations of something pleasant. An unexpected bonus. A small gift, perhaps. Or discovering the first daffodil in bloom beneath the huge old copper beech tree, as she and Livvy had done only yesterday. Or even finding that a young patient was doing better than expected on a chosen course of treatment.

It certainly wasn't being faced with a man Hannah had had no expectations of ever seeing again. A man who had no knowledge of the very real and solid connection he had with her life. A man who had the potential to cause untold damage if he learned about that connection now. This was no surprise. It was a shock. A stunning blow that was now causing a horrible crawling sensation through Hannah's limbs as its paralysing effects wore off. It took only another split second to realise she was in command of her facial features again and Hannah hoped that the cool smile she summoned would cover up her initial response to this encounter.

'It certainly is a surprise,' she murmured. 'How are you, Jack?'

'Surprised.' Dark brown eyes were regarding Hannah with a faintly wary expression. Was he waiting for a signal of some kind? Or was the 'surprise' as unpleasant from his side as it was from Hannah's? 'I've spent the last few years imagining you living in Auckland,' he added. A question was lurking in those dark eyes now but Hannah was not about to answer it. What could she say, anyway? That she had turned the job offer down because the thought of working in close proximity to him had been too offputting?

Peter had watched the brief exchange with raised eyebrows and a grin that indicated at least one person found this encounter a pleasant surprise. 'You two know each other,' he said unnecessarily. 'This is great. As friendly faces in this department go, Jack, Hannah is top of the list.'

'I'm sure she is.' Jack's observation was polite but definitely reserved.

'We don't know each other *that* well.' Hannah was finally able to drag her gaze away from Jack's face. To stop the unconscious catalogue of the minor changes that five years had wrought. A little grey amongst the dark brown curls that were shorter than they used to be. A network of fine lines at the corners of those deceptively warm eyes. A subtle change in the overall relationship between his features that gave the impression that Jack Douglas had done a lot of living in the last five years and that tears as well as laughter had been involved. She stamped firmly on the twinge of curiosity that surfaced. She didn't want to know. 'We met briefly, a few years ago.' Hannah kept her words directed at Peter. 'We were both applying for positions at the same hospital.'

What did Jack mean, he had been imagining her working in Auckland? National Children's Hospital was large but not large enough to simply not notice a member of staff for years. She was able to look at Jack again now without revealing anything more than a polite interest. 'Have you had enough of the "City of Sails", then?'

'I didn't take the surgical residency in Auckland,'

Jack responded. 'I was called back to England and had to remain there due to family commitments.'

Ah, yes...the *family* commitments. The family Jack had denied having. No wife, he had confirmed blithely when Hannah had specifically asked. No kids. And she had believed him. The recollection of her gullibility made her tone tight.

'And you've brought your family with you this time?'

'Of course.'

'Jack has a son,' Peter informed Hannah. 'He's seven.'

'How nice.' Hannah's smile was as tight as her tone. *As if she didn't know.* 'He should enjoy living here.'

'He's a bit older than Livvy,' Peter added sociably.

'Who's Livvy?' Jack queried.

'Olivia...my daughter,' Hannah was forced to respond. So much for hoping to avoid this area of her personal life, but maybe it was just as well to get it out of the way. Alarm that she might not succeed in letting Jack know this was none of his business made her tone sharp, but it was impossible to speak of Olivia without an emotional response and her smile loosened just a little.

'How old is Olivia?'

The alarm bells clamoured with more urgency. If Hannah told the truth then Jack would probably put two and two together in a matter of moments. They had been together just over five years ago. Olivia would turn five in a few months. It was hardly rocket science.

Peter filled the fractional gap with ease. 'She's just a wee dot,' he said warmly. 'Seems like only yesterday she was born. How long ago was it, Hannah? Three years?'

Bless Peter's vagueness about anything personal

rather than professional. Hannah's smile was far more relaxed this time. 'She's four,' she said. 'Just,' she added hurriedly, for good measure.

She could see the lightning-fast calculations going on in Jack's mind, and she saw the flash of what could have been pain cross his features momentarily. She welcomed the sense of being in control it gave her. The last time she had felt in control like this had been the moment she'd walked out on Jack and taken charge of her life to prevent history repeating itself. Hannah had coped then and she was damned well going to cope now.

Jack's expression hardened and it was easy to see what he was thinking. She had gone from him straight into the arms of another man. What they had had together had meant nothing to her. Hannah lifted her chin. Why should she care what he thought of her? Far better to believe that than learn the truth.

'Excuse me.' The approach of Caroline Briggs made Hannah realise that they were blocking a significant portion of the corridor and her scattered papers were littering the only available route past. 'I don't want to tread on anything important.'

Some of the papers were copies from Jadine's file and Hannah didn't want Caroline to think that her daughter's privacy was unprotected. She stooped hurriedly to rescue some of the paperwork. 'Sorry, Caroline. We're a bit in the way here, aren't we?'

'No problem. Can I help?'

'I'll manage.' Hannah glanced up to smile at Caroline. 'Are you heading home now?'

'I'm off to the hairdresser, actually.' Caroline looked a little defensive. 'I might even get my nails done. Jadie's sound asleep so there didn't seem much point in waiting.'

'Sounds like a good idea,' Hannah said reassuringly. She couldn't help noticing her own nails as she reached for another sheet of paper. Short and practical, they were as bare of any colour as her fingers were of rings. One nail was badly broken, thanks to having to fix the blockage in that pipe that fed the water trough last weekend. She hadn't noticed what a contrast they presented to Caroline's hands. Jadine's mother's fingertips looked as though a session at a beauty salon was not an unusual experience. 'Enjoy your night out,' she added. 'And don't worry about Jadine. We'll call you if there's any change.'

Peter watched Caroline as she walked away from them. 'That's the mother of our frequent flyer, isn't it?'

Hannah nodded. She picked up the last of her papers and shoved them into the side pocket of her briefcase. Glancing up, she caught sight of Caroline's back as she waited for the lift. The curls in her blond hair also advertised careful maintenance but the dark line at the roots suggested that putting off an appointment might have been inconvenient. Especially with an important date lined up tonight.

The less than charitable thought was uncharacteristic enough to astonish Hannah. Had Jack's appearance rattled her enough to provoke such an unprofessionally judgmental attitude? Or was it more that he had made her aware of her own appearance? Could he see the extra lines that the years had undoubtedly etched into her own face? At least she had no grey hairs visibly lightening the dark honey blond, but compared to Caroline's Hannah's hair was as boring as her nails. Dragged back into a practical ponytail, the dead straight tresses were only this long because Hannah couldn't be bothered going to a hairdresser very often. The uncomfortable ability to see herself as Jack probably did made it difficult to concentrate on what Peter was saying.

'Any reason to suspect this visit is genuine?'

'Oh, I think it's genuine enough,' Hannah responded. 'I'm just not convinced that it's medical. I think I'll take your advice and bring the psych services in on this one.'

Jack had been watching Caroline enter the lift and Hannah found a curiosity she thought she had extinguished years ago resurface. What was his wife like? Carefully groomed, she suspected, as befitted a surgeon's partner. No broken nails for her and no schoolgirl hairstyle tied with one of her daughter's scrunchies which sported a bright red teddy-bear ornament. Peter had only mentioned the child she'd already known about so maybe Jack and his wife hadn't been lucky enough to add a daughter to their family. Well, he would just have to do without, in that case. No way was he going to lay any claim to Livvy.

'Are the psych services intended for the mother or the child?' Jack's interest was courteous but Hannah had no desire to continue this conversation. Shades of her talk with Caroline earlier today about the difficulties of being a solo parent were haunting her now but instead of feeling proud of having coped so well by herself Hannah was aware of a rapidly building resentment.

It was because of this man standing in front of her that she had had to fight to keep her career alive. Had struggled to keep a roof over her head and pay the bills and keep herself and Livvy clothed and fed. She had managed to get through the episodes of illness, including that nasty dose of chickenpox last year. Had survived countless sleepless nights with a tiny baby and the worries of new parenthood without the kind of relief or simply support a loving partner could have provided. Life

over the last five years—and for the foreseeable future—
would have been very different indeed if it hadn't been
for Jack Douglas.

'Possibly for the doctor at this rate,' she said lightly
in response to Jack's query. 'You'll have to excuse me
but I don't want to be late collecting my daughter from
day care.'

'You use *day care*?' Jack's interest was not merely
courteous now. It was focused and intense enough to
make Hannah grit her teeth. She had come across this
kind of prejudice often enough, but to have it come from
the person who had created the need for it in her life
was enough to push her past any intended boundaries of
staying politely aloof.

'I have a career as well as a child.' Hannah knew that
at some point in the very near future she would admire
the control she was managing to achieve right now. 'I
don't find them to be mutually exclusive despite the fact
that I'm a woman.'

'I didn't mean to—'

'I'm sure you didn't.' Hannah's interruption was as
smooth as it was forceful. Her gaze was locked on Jack's
so it was safe enough to let him know that her mood in
no way matched her words…or her tone. 'And I'm sure
you don't intend to hold me up any longer. Enjoy the
rest of your tour.' She turned away, deliberately cutting
off any attempt Jack might have made to say anything
else. 'Catch you tomorrow, Pete. 8 a.m. start for the ward
round?'

'Sounds good. Have a great evening.'

Hannah was already walking away. Every step was
going to take her farther away from Jack. Her evening
was getting better already.

The improvement continued. Hannah could feel her

spirits lifting as she hurried along the ground-level corridor past Orthopaedic Outpatients and the plaster room on her right, the hospital pharmacy and chaplain's office to her left. A sharp turn just before the entrance to the bone marrow transplant unit took her through a door into a fire-exit stairwell that was a short cut to the main car parking area for staff. Now she just had to negotiate the route past the hospital kitchens, Medical Records and the pathology department. Hannah kept up her brisk pace, trying to shake off the remnants of her reaction to seeing Jack again. The beginnings of the smile that tugged at her lips had a hint of smugness. If he tried to follow one of her private routes around this hospital he would get lost in no time at all.

If only she hadn't got lost trying to find her way around that unfamiliar and huge children's hospital in Auckland all those years ago. Dressed to the nines in a tailored skirt and jacket, nervously clutching the same briefcase she held now and panicking just a little. She had only scant minutes left to find the venue for her interview, and the sign hanging from the ceiling ahead of her indicated she had still not found the general medicine office suite.

He had been standing just beneath the unhelpful sign, wearing a suit and apparently absorbed in reading the contents of a manila folder. There had been a faint air of tension about him as though he'd been reading something important. Or waiting for someone who was late showing up. There had also been an aura of assurance. He'd obviously belonged there. He'd looked like a doctor. He would know where General Medicine was.

So Hannah approached him. Her determination to find her own way and handle the nerve-racking process of applying for her first permanent job with aplomb had been replaced by a desire to avoid looking stupid by arriving late and confessing she hadn't been able to find her way. The solitary man beneath the sign seemed to be her best chance of resolving her predicament. She had cleared her throat to attract his attention away from the folder.

'Excuse me. I'm wondering if you might be able to help me?'

He'd looked up from the folder and Hannah found herself the new focus of a pair of the darkest…and warmest brown eyes she had ever seen.

'That would be a pleasure.' The frown line between the unusually dark eyes disappeared and then the man smiled and Hannah knew that the conviction she had cemented over the last year that she had lost the capacity to find men attractive was completely wrong. The totally unexpected and badly timed realisation was disconcerting and Hannah dragged her gaze away from the disarming smile only to find it caught again by those dark, dark eyes. She could see a distinctly amused gleam in them now.

'*How* can I help?'

'I…ah…' Hannah caught her bottom lip between her teeth, unhappily aware that she was probably compounding an image of being a helpless female. Not only had she been unable to follow directions but she was now rendered incoherent by the smile from a good-looking man. There was only one way out before this got any worse and Hannah took it. She smiled wryly as she made her confession. 'I'm kind of lost.'

'I'm not surprised. This is a very large hospital.'

Hannah's deep breath was almost a sigh of relief. She didn't feel so stupid any more. His tone was understanding. Sympathetic. And he had an accent. English, but not the public-school variety. It was more of a lilt that added colour to an already attractively deep voice.

'Where are you heading?'

'General Medicine. Not the ward, though. I'm looking for the head of department's office.' The movement to push her wrist clear of her navy jacket sleeve and check her watch was automatic. 'I've got a job interview in five minutes.'

'Have you?' Thick, dark eyebrows rose until they almost vanished beneath the wayward curls above. 'What's the job?'

'A registrar's position. It's the first one I've ever applied for and I really don't want to be late.' The words tumbled out. This was no time to be distracted into conversation no matter how attractive this stranger was. 'Look, I'm getting a bit desperate here. Can you help me?'

'I'd love to.' The sincerity in the statement was obvious. 'But…I'm afraid I can't.'

Hannah held back a renewed surge of panic. 'What?'

'I hate to admit this…but I'm as lost as you are.'

'*What?*' Hannah knew she probably looked like a fish stranded out of water but she didn't care. She had just wasted another precious two minutes and she was no closer to finding her goal.

'I've got a job interview myself.' The explanation was apologetic. 'For a surgical consultancy. First one I've ever applied for as well and I'm damned if I can read this map and find the department.'

They stared at each other.

And then they laughed.

The tension evaporated by magic then and they both studied the map in the manila folder together. The stranger's hand touched Hannah's and she decided it really didn't matter if she was a minute or two late. He was going to be even later for his appointment because he insisted on taking the stairs to the next level and making sure Hannah had found her destination.

'Good luck,' he'd said finally. He paused as he turned away. 'I'm Jack, by the way. Jack Douglas.'

'I'm Hannah Campbell,' she responded. 'And thanks. Good luck to you, too.'

The charm of that encounter hung around Hannah. Quite apart from being devastatingly attractive, Jack Douglas had been so *nice*. He had gone out of his way to help her despite needing help himself. And he had made her laugh when she'd been feeling anything but relaxed. The combination had created a magic that had stayed with Hannah well after the door had closed again behind him.

She slammed the car door with unnecessary vigour but a punctuation point was definitely in order. There was no point in raking over old coals and Hannah had left the remains of that blaze alone for so long now she was surprised to find the memory so vivid. Maybe if she'd been prepared for seeing Jack again she could have thrown some extra protection into place. On the other hand, maybe letting things surface so that she could deal with them once and for all was healthier. The reminder of an important lesson, no matter how well learned, was never a complete waste of time or energy.

And the worst was over now. She had seen Jack Douglas again. Had acknowledged that he looked and sounded pretty much the same. And she hadn't been attracted. Not one tiny bit. The relief she'd experienced walking away from him had been palpable. It was still

with her now twenty minutes later as she walked towards
the old converted villa that housed the Maysfield Child
Care Centre. The moment she walked inside and saw
her daughter, the resolve that she would never let anything—or anyone—threaten what they had was strength-
ened to the point where Hannah felt invincible. She
would deal with this because there was simply no other
choice.

'Mummy!' A small face shone with delight and
Hannah held out her arms to catch Olivia's headlong
rush. 'I made you something, Mummy. You can *eat* it.'

'Fabulous. I'm starving.' Hannah hoped it wasn't a
sand pie decorated with marigold petals like the one she
had been presented with in the sandpit last week.

'It's quite safe.' Shirley Smith, the owner-operator of
the child care centre, grinned at Hannah. 'We've been
in the kitchen this afternoon.'

'They're butterfly cakes, Mummy. Come and *look*!
They're be-yootiful.'

Hannah had to agree. The tops of the Madeira cake
muffins had been sliced off and halved, to be positioned
in the icing later as wings. Jelly beans had made col-
ourful bodies and feelers had been created from tiny
strips of liquorice.

'I made two, Mummy. One for you and one for me.'

'Shall we save them for later? A special treat for sup-
per?' Hannah could see the battle the decision-making
process caused but her smile was automatic. Had she
really never noticed before how similar Olivia's eyes
were to her father's? Perhaps the fact that they were
framed by blond hair had made the comparison less obvious. And she had never credited her daughter's curls
to Jack either. She was just Livvy—her gorgeous, lov-
able and incredibly precious child. Impulsively, she

gathered the small body into her arms again and kissed the soft, fluffy curls. 'Thank you for making me a butterfly cake, darling. Love you.'

'Love you, too.' Olivia wriggled free. 'Let's go home, Mummy. I want to count the daff-dils.'

Shirley walked out to the car-parking area with them. 'Did you see the van?'

'No. Has it arrived, then?' Hannah looked around at Shirley's smile. She must have been very preoccupied on her arrival not to spot the minibus parked in the corner. The paint job with the centre's name surrounded by bright cartoon characters was eye-catching. 'It looks great!'

'We're going to start the school runs next week.'

'I'm so pleased.' Hannah lifted Olivia onto her booster seat in the back of the car and fastened her safety belt. 'I was dreading having to make other arrangements when Livvy starts school.' The centre's hours of 7 a.m. to 7 p.m. had been brilliant for Hannah and after nearly four years of coming here it was a second home for Olivia. The staff were caring and Shirley was a firm part of the family now.

'I'm not sure about the roster for driving yet. I think Lucy's a bit young at nineteen but some of the others are just as keen. I'm also having to decide how many schools we open the service to. I don't want numbers to climb too much.'

Hannah nodded. Olivia had been one of the first clients of Shirley's business. The numbers had climbed steadily over the years but there were never more than about twenty children at any one time. If too many parents took advantage of having the hours before and after school catered for then the atmosphere of the centre might change.

'Just don't leave Maysfield Primary off the list. Livvy's enrolled there.'

'That's the closest school so it'll be first. It may be enough by itself for the moment. I might wait and see what the numbers are like.' Shirley leaned into the car to give Olivia a kiss. 'Bye, sweetheart. See you tomorrow.'

Olivia balanced the small box containing the butterfly cakes on her knee and chattered non-stop until they arrived home. Hannah parked her small hatchback outside the old stable and then released her daughter, who ran straight to where the copper beech was unfurling its bright, velvety new leaves. She crouched amongst the numerous spears of green foliage beneath the tree and the triumphant shout made Hannah grin. Olivia knew her numbers perfectly well, she was just too excited to take the time needed to recite them all in order.

'One, two, four, seven...nine. There's *nine* daff-dils now, Mummy.'

'Would you like to pick some to take in for Shirley tomorrow?'

'Ooh, yes. I *love* picking flowers.'

'I know.' Hannah didn't mind that the golden blooms would vanish. There were plenty more buds ready to open and take their place. And it didn't matter that the flowers were beheaded without much stalk length. Shirley was bound to have a short jam jar to put them in. The pleasure of watching Olivia's face as she concentrated on making yet another gift was too great to interfere with. Did other children gain such intense satisfaction from giving? Hannah doubted it. Olivia was special. Such a happy, loving little girl that she could only enhance the lives of anyone privileged enough to know her.

'Let's put them in some water for now.' Hannah led the way beneath the ancient wisteria vine that festooned the bull-nosed verandah of the 1860s cottage. The narrow hallway led past the original four rooms with their glowing kauri flooring and joinery which Hannah had painstakingly stripped of countless layers of paint. It finished at the north-facing addition to the cottage that had been a celebration of gaining her senior registrar post at Christchurch Central. The inadequate lean-to kitchen and bathroom facilities had been replaced and the kitchen she and Olivia entered now was a sunny, open space with a dining area to one side of French doors leading to a bricked courtyard garden.

Two cats, one completely black and the other white, were waiting patiently near the fridge.

'Hello, Sooty. Hello, Snow.' Olivia dropped to a crouch again to haul each cat into her arms for a cuddle that was gentle enough to be well received.

Hannah rescued the abandoned daffodils and put them into a glass of water. She looked up to find Olivia's face sporting an expression remarkably similar to Sooty's and Snow's.

'I'm hungry, Mummy. Can I have a biscuit?'

'It's nearly dinnertime, darling.'

'Please?'

'Just one, then. I'm going to get changed and then we can go and feed the hens.'

'Can I make a sandwich for Joe?'

'Joe doesn't need a sandwich, pet. He's getting fat. Sandwiches should really only be special treats for donkeys.'

'*We're* going to have a special treat later.'

Hannah smiled. 'So we are. I'd almost forgotten about

the butterfly cakes. OK, then. Joe can have a sandwich
but just one slice of bread and not too much Marmite.'

Hannah kicked off her court shoes and unzipped her
skirt, reaching for the faded denim jeans hanging over
the end of the brass bedstead in her room. A soft, well-
worn polo-necked jersey covered the shirt she had worn
to work and she sat on the bed to pull on the warm socks
she would need inside her gumboots. This was her favourite time of the day. She could stop being professional and sink into the comfort of being where she most
loved to be with the person she most wanted to be with.
It was bliss.

The fine woollen skirt needed some cat hair brushed
off before being hung in the wardrobe but Hannah took
the time to care for the garment. It had lasted for years
now, as had many of her good-quality clothes. Flicking
through the hangers in the wardrobe was no more than
a random gesture. She couldn't pretend she was looking
to see if it was still there because she had known all
along that it was. Why had she even kept that white
gypsy blouse with its rainbow drawstring neck? She'd
never worn it again and it was hardly likely to come
back into fashion.

It had been a relief to get changed that day as well. To
escape the restrictions of that tailored suit and head out
for a walk to celebrate a successful end to a stressful
day and to explore this exciting city. As usual, Hannah
had been wearing a favourite pair of jeans and the pretty
gypsy top had been perfect for the glorious summer
weather Auckland had turned on. The motel she'd been
staying in near the hospital had been central enough for
the vibrancy of New Zealand's largest city to surround
it and high enough to give tantalising glimpses of the

Waitemata Harbour with its spectacular bridge and the holiday atmosphere the yachting activity provided. Auckland had been a totally new city for Hannah and she'd known she would love it if she was lucky enough to get the job and come there to live. The fact that her interview had gone so well made the possibility of starting a new life very real and the excitement the prospect generated made Hannah feel happier than she had in a very long time.

The coffee was great, too. A hot, creamy, strong latté in an outdoor café that had an unobstructed view of a large patch of harbour. Hannah was more than happy to sit by herself and enjoy the last part of the afternoon. She was even happier, however, at the interruption.

'Excuse me, but I'm wondering if you might be able to help me?'

Hannah was laughing even before she turned towards the source of the instantly recognisable voice.

'I'm looking for a good cup of coffee.' Jack kept his face straight for a few seconds longer. 'Can you recommend this establishment?'

The coffee was so good that Hannah had another one. It shouldn't really have seemed like fate stepping in that Jack was staying at the same nearby motel. It was, after all, the closest one to the hospital and had been top of the recommended list. It was also coincidental that Jack's interview had gone well and that, like Hannah, he was now on the shortlist for a coveted position; and it was hardly a surprise that they were both visiting Auckland for the first time. It seemed only polite to share the celebration of a satisfying day and completely logical to join forces and spend the evening exploring a little of the city.

'After all,' Jack pointed out, 'we wouldn't want to get lost, would we?'

They shouldn't really have stayed out so late when they both had a second round of interviews the next day. And they probably shouldn't have visited the Stardome Observatory on One Tree Hill as they finally headed back towards their motel. If they hadn't already identified the constellations through the giant telescope inside, they wouldn't have lain on a deserted, grassy slope later, trying to find them again.

And Jack wouldn't have kissed her. Or had she kissed him? It didn't matter. The attraction between them was so mutual and so strong that Hannah barely registered the breaking of so many of her private rules regarding men. She was about to start a new life here. Everything was new and exciting and tinged with a magic she had never encountered before. What better way to make it memorable for ever than to spend a night with the most wonderful man she had ever met? Reckless? Yes. Memorable?

Oh, very definitely, yes. Far too memorable. Hannah pushed the wardrobe door shut and made sure the latch clicked. Maybe she couldn't stem the flow but she could shut these disturbing memories away again just as quickly. They just needed airing. A quick shake and then they could go back where they had come from and lie undisturbed, hopefully for good this time.

Olivia's fluorescent pink gumboots looked positively lurid as they caught the last of the sunshine. Joseph, the grey donkey, was duly appreciative of the mangled piece of bread and Marmite. Velvety lips carefully plucked the offering from the tiny hand Hannah held flat on top of her own. She rubbed inside the length of the shaggy ear and Joseph closed his eyes and lowered his head in ecstasy. Olivia planted a noisy kiss on his nose.

'We have to go now, Joe,' she told their largest pet. 'We have to see if the eggs have cracked.'

Arthur, the Chinese Silky bantam rooster, was strutting proudly in front of the henhouse with Bianca, Carla and Elsa close by. Deirdre was inside, as she had been for over a week now, keeping her clutch of six eggs warm. She appeared as Hannah scattered handfuls of grain and Olivia's blond curls almost disappeared as she poked her head into the nesting box for a closer look.

'There's no cracks yet, Mummy.'

'I think it takes a bit longer than a week for them to hatch.'

'Maybe tomorrow?'

'Maybe.' Hannah squeezed the small hand that slid into hers as they headed back to the house via a quick visit to shift Horace the goat's tethering pole. 'We'll have to think up some names for the chickens when they hatch, won't we? What's the next letter after "E"?'

Olivia had to think hard about that. She sang her way through the alphabet song as she pulled off the pink gumboots.

'F,' she declared finally.

'Good girl! What sound does "F" make?'

'Fffff.'

'So what will we call the first chicken? Fiona? Felicity?' Hannah hunted in the pantry to find some tomato paste to make Olivia's favourite pasta dish for dinner.

'Fred.'

'Hmm. Arthur won't be very happy if we have a boy chicken.'

'Why not?'

'Because he'll grow up into another rooster and they might fight.'

'Why?'

'Because roosters like to have the hens all to themselves.'

'Why?'

'That's just the way roosters are. They don't like sharing. Can you find some plates, darling? Our dinner will be ready soon and then it'll be time for your bath and a story.'

Olivia shook her head sadly. 'You almost forgot again, Mummy.'

'What did I almost forget, darling?'

'The butterfly cakes.'

Hannah smiled. 'No way. I wouldn't forget anything that important.'

Olivia's happy smile showed she had no idea her mother was not being entirely truthful. She *had* forgotten about the butterfly cakes. It was just a shame she couldn't choose some other things to forget. Still, if she could pretend well enough to convince her daughter and keep her happy, maybe she could pretend well enough to convince herself and avoid some misery.

More importantly, she could convince Jack Douglas that nothing of any importance had ever happened between them.

And never could.

CHAPTER THREE

'HAVE you considered hydrostatic reduction?'

'That would only be appropriate if the history was for less than twenty-four hours and there were no signs of peritonitis. Daniel's temperature is rising and there was some evidence of bloodstained mucus in the last nappy change. I wouldn't have called you if I didn't think a surgical reduction was urgent.'

'You're probably quite correct,' Jack said mildly. 'But that shouldn't prevent us discussing the possibility of less invasive treatment, should it? How high is his temperature?'

'Thirty-seven point eight.'

'Not exactly a raging fever, then. Was the bloodstained mucus obvious or detected by lab results?'

'Lab results.' Hannah had to make a conscious effort not to let her tone rise defensively.

'And how long is it since the first symptoms were apparent?'

'Twenty-six hours.'

'So it could be considered borderline for conservative rather than surgical management, wouldn't you agree?'

'No, I wouldn't,' Hannah said coolly. 'Daniel Chubb presented with classic symptoms for intussusception. He was inconsolable for periods, would go pale and then have a period of normality before repeating the sequence. Unfortunately the GP saw him during a normal spell. He was brought in by ambulance an hour ago when he started vomiting during the crying spells. He has a sausage-shaped mass palpable in the right upper abdomen and the abdominal X-ray showed a mass and an absent gas pattern over the caecum and ascending colon. The ultrasound confirmed an ileocolic intussusception. I would prefer to avoid any further delay in treatment. Established peritonitis in a two-year-old child is a serious complication.'

Jack met the implacable glare he was receiving with an inward sigh. He wasn't about to argue the merits of rushing this baby into surgery. The investigations had been appropriate and the diagnosis was undoubtedly spot on. Having been called in for a surgical opinion, however, it would have been nice to have been allowed to offer one rather than be presented with the patient and told what he needed to do. Not that there was any point in discussing the issue. Hannah Campbell had made up her mind and because her judgement in this case was perfectly justified it would be a waste of time and possibly detrimental to their young patient to try and make a point regarding her attitude.

But it was more than irritating. Jack loosened his tie and removed it twenty minutes later, looping it over the hook in his locker in the theatre changing room before starting on his shirt buttons. Daniel Chubb was the third case referred to him from Hannah Campbell's paediatric firm since he had started working at Christchurch Central Hospital ten days ago. Given their past association, some teething problems in establishing a professional relationship with Hannah were only to be expected but his hope that the situation would improve quickly was clearly overly ambitious. If anything, it was deteriorating.

The first, straightforward case of an umbilical hernia repair in a six-month-old infant had been only two days after that rather tense meeting outside Hannah's office.

The early morning, pre-operative visit to the ward had been a courtesy rather than a necessity and, having been directed to the ward's playroom, Jack had certainly not expected to find his otherwise perfectly healthy patient in the care of a senior registrar rather than a parent. The playroom was a large, well-stocked area on the north side of the hospital wing. The huge windows that provided the lovely view of the park and river outside also allowed sunshine to stream in and highlight the rainbow of colours of the soft furnishings and toys in the room. The area had suddenly seemed an entirely appropriate setting in which to find Hannah, and Jack's pause to absorb the scene had been involuntary.

Hannah stood near the windows, holding the baby on one hip as she chatted to him, the soft musical intonation of her speech clearly finding a fascinated audience. 'See the ducks, Jason? Look at that one diving for his breakfast. What sound do ducks make?' She smiled at the baby. 'Quack, quack!' The imitation was unselfconsciously enthusiastic and baby Jason grinned back, flapped his hands and gurgled his appreciation.

Hannah hadn't noticed Jack standing in the doorway and he hadn't moved a muscle. He had noted on their first meeting that five years had done little to diminish the young doctor's physical attractions but it hadn't occurred to him they might, in fact, have increased. Her height accentuated a slender figure that motherhood had not altered and the sunlight seemed to have been captured by the threads of gold in her hair. It was longer these days, and the ponytail was not particularly alluring but it was all too easy to imagine what it would be like allowed to hang loose to drift around her shoulders and soften the determined line of that jaw.

The softly flared skirt and low-heeled shoes didn't

quite fit the picture either. Jack's memories of Hannah always put her in faded jeans and that flimsy white top with the pretty string that had been so inviting to loosen. As inviting as slipping his hand below the gaping neckline to find the soft fullness of breasts that had been as eager for his touch as her lips had been.

Jack moved now but not any further into the playroom. He turned sharply and went back towards the ward office. Increasing the space between himself and Hannah was necessary to counter both the unwanted memory and his body's physical reaction to it. The tightening in his groin was disturbing enough to make Jack set his mouth in a very uncharacteristically grim line. He had been so sure he was well past any influence Hannah could exert on him. He had eventually dismissed her from his life with the same resolution with which he had embarked on becoming a parent for his son. It had only been a momentary blip in his life history, for heaven's sake. A purely physical encounter that he had absolutely no desire to revisit despite any treacherous suggestions his body might have to offer.

Pulling the white theatre gumboots onto his feet, Jack took a hat from the box by the door as he moved towards the scrub room. The distance had certainly helped at the time. As had a weekend's break before the second case he'd had to work on with Hannah. Her apparently deliberate rudeness in directing the presentation of that case to his registrar rather than himself had also been helpful. Awareness of the putdown had made any repetition of a flash of physical awareness highly unlikely.

Her voice had had nothing of the alluring quality that attracted babies either. It had been clipped. Professional and cool.

'James presented with a ''near miss cot-death'' episode at four weeks of age. He was monitored carefully but was readmitted a few weeks later due to his GP's concern at his failure to thrive. A barium swallow and endoscopy have confirmed the gastro-oesophageal reflux which, so far, hasn't responded to conservative management. As you can see, his weight gain over the last two weeks hasn't been significant.'

It was Jack who was reading through the notes. His registrar, Barry Portman, was too busy hanging onto every word Hannah was uttering.

'Any further episodes of apnoea?'

'No, but he did have a witnessed period of near syncopy with bradycardia yesterday.' The glance Hannah directed at Jack was unquestionably challenging. 'Presumably vagus nerve mediated as a result of the reflux.'

'You've tried medications like a proton pump inhibitor?''

'Of course.'

It wasn't necessary to go over every detail of the management Hannah's firm had put in place over the infant's admission but Jack was pleased to find he could interact with Hannah on that occasion without provoking even a hint of any unwelcome physical response. And the more he picked over the details the more he could see the cracks in Dr Campbell's intelligent and professional façade. She couldn't stand the sight of him on a personal level, and that was fine by him.

Quite contagious, in fact. The degree of antipathy towards each other was rapidly becoming just as mutual as that ill-advised initial attraction had been. While it would be far easier to foster the negative atmosphere than achieve tolerance, Jack had made yet another effort when called in to see Daniel Chubb that morning. And he'd had his effort thrown straight back at him.

Jack scrubbed his hands with meticulous attention to both technique and thoroughness as he prepared to enter the operating theatre. He had been quite prepared to co-operate with the paediatric department's most senior registrar on a professional level without letting any personal opinions interfere with either of them being able to perform their jobs well, but Hannah was making it totally impossible.

Having completed scrubbing around his nails, Jack moved the small brush to the hollows between the knuckles and then started on his forearms. Allowing Hannah to continue to treat him this way was unacceptable, both professionally and personally. He didn't appreciate the rather patronising tolerance she was subjecting him to and he wasn't going to tolerate her brick-wall approach to having her opinions questioned in any way. He knew better than anyone that Dr Campbell was capable of misjudging a situation and that having made up her mind she then closed it with a finality that precluded any possibility of persuading her otherwise.

Jack rinsed his hands, holding them down to let the water flow from his wrists to his fingertips, then angling them up to change the direction of the flow to run from his wrists to his elbows. Shoving the tap off with a practised nudge from his elbow, Jack picked up the sterile towel from the package lying open on the bench beside him. A theatre nurse stood nearby, holding a gown ready for him to put on over his scrub suit. Jack nodded his thanks as he pushed his arms into the sleeves of the gown. He found he was able to shake off the last of his irritation as the nurse tied the strings at the back of the gown. Hannah was not about to undermine his concentration on the task at hand.

He had come to terms with her less than desirable personality attributes a long time ago, after all. He'd come to believe, quite sincerely, that he'd probably had a lucky escape. The problem was that he'd never expected to have to deal with her in a professional capacity and while an errant memory of her physical attractions had been easy enough to dismiss, the prospect of continued association was still disturbing because her tendency to close her mind had the potential to be dangerous. Fortunately, it hadn't been dangerous in young Daniel Chubb's case. In fact, delaying surgery to attempt more conservative medical treatment could have presented a far more rocky road to recovery.

The impacted intestinal obstruction had been caused by a Meckel's diverticulum, a common gastro-intestinal tract anomaly. This one was large enough to require a limited small bowel resection and was close enough to perforation to justify the IV antibiotic course Hannah had already instigated before Daniel had left the ward. Jack worked carefully on his tiny patient, using crushing clamps to isolate the affected area before dividing it clear. His registrar was ready to pick up the clamps.

'Bring the two ends of the bowel together,' Jack instructed, 'and now gently turn the clamps back on themselves. I'm going to join the adjacent walls of the small bowel with a seromuscular Lembert suture.' He stitched quietly for a minute or two before speaking again. 'See what I'm doing on the corner here?'

'Is that a Connell suture?'

Jack grinned. 'OK, I'm impressed. Do you want to finish this?'

'Sure.' Barry took the needle holders, securing the double-ended suture, and stepped into the position Jack had been in. Jack watched the surgical registrar closely, pleased to observe the younger man's deftness and attention to detail.

'That's great,' he said finally. 'Next time you can try the resection as well.'

'Cool.'

The atmosphere in Theatre was relaxed now. Jack was only starting to get to know all the staff but he had been astonished by how welcoming and friendly they had been so far. Rather a dramatic contrast to the reception he was getting from some quarters in the paediatric ward.

'How's the hunt for a nanny going, Jack?' The query came from the anaesthetist, Shona. 'Was that agency I recommended any use?'

Jack nodded. 'I meant to thank you for that, Shona.' At least someone had gone out of their way to be helpful on such an urgent issue. He'd wanted to ask Hannah about the kind of day care she used for her daughter on his first day here but she had practically bitten his head off. 'I've employed someone from their books but I'm not sure how it's going to work out yet. She's very young and Ben says she spends a lot of time on the phone, presumably to her boyfriend.'

'How old is Ben?'

'Seven. It's not as though he needs constant watching.' Jack leaned closer to see what Barry was doing. 'Put interrupted sutures in the mesenteric defect to close it, Barry. And be careful not to pick up any mesenteric vessels.' He kept watching the suturing as he continued his conversation with Shona. 'This nanny, Lisa, is only nineteen and she's doing some varsity units which clash a bit with after-school hours.'

'Sounds like that might be a problem.'

'Doesn't seem to be. I think I got lucky with the

school we chose. There's a day care agency that's just started an after-school pick-up service from Maysfield Primary so Ben's going there a few days a week and Lisa collects him after her lectures and takes him home. The extra cost involved is more than made up for by the fact she's willing to stay overnight when I'm on call. She's quite keen on making it a live-in position if things work out.'

'Must be tough,' Barry murmured. 'Being a single dad.'

'It's getting easier as Ben gets older,' Jack responded. 'And I wouldn't be without him, that's for sure.'

'No.' Shona's voice was soft as she traced a finger across the forehead of the baby she was monitoring carefully. 'They're rather precious, these wee guys.' She glanced up. 'Are we nearly finished?'

'Yes.' Jack could see that Barry was ready to start the final suturing. 'We're up to skin level.'

'Good. I'll start waking him up.'

Jack watched the baby being carried from the theatre only minutes later as he stripped off his gown and gloves. Shona was right. Sons *were* precious. Ben hadn't been any older than Daniel when he'd been admitted to hospital that first time and if it hadn't been for the disasters that had occurred as a result of that admission he might never have known he even had a son.

How different life would have been. Jack wouldn't have hesitated in taking the position he'd been offered in Auckland. The prospect had been mind-blowingly exciting and it hadn't mattered that the excitement had had more to do with Hannah Campbell than the job on offer. She had been just as excited. As soon as they had congratulated each other on their success, plans for the future had tumbled forth. They would need a few weeks

to tidy up their former lives and then they could be together—maybe for ever, the way things had appeared to
be shaping up. They didn't want to part for that long,
mind you. Hannah had started juggling phone calls, trying to delay her flight so they could have an extra night
together, and Jack had gone out for take-aways. The purchase of a bottle of champagne had prolonged his absence but it had seemed an essential addition to the
planned evening. They were going to celebrate the new
lives they were heading towards and Jack, at least, was
intending to celebrate finding what he was convinced
was the love of his life.

He'd been smitten from the moment he'd looked up
from trying to decipher that stupid map and had found
himself faced with a pair of deep blue eyes that had
advertised the intelligence of their owner and her embarrassment in asking for assistance when so determined
to cope by herself. When she had laughed at finding he'd
been in the same predicament, the strength of his attraction had been sealed. On top of her intelligence and determination, she had a sense of humour. *And* she was
gorgeous. *And* she was as attracted to him as he was to
her. Fate had brought them together, not once but twice.
Jack hadn't been able to believe his luck when he'd spotted her drinking coffee in that café when he'd gone out
for a stroll at the end of his day. They were destined to
be together.

Ha! Jack made a detour to his office so he could dic-
tate the operative notes on Daniel Chubb while they
were still fresh in his mind. It took a minute or two
before he could concentrate on using his Dictaphone,
however. Even now, he could feel the faint echo of the
astonishment he had experienced when he'd arrived back
at the motel unit that night, carrying steaming trays of

Chinese food and an icy bottle of expensive French champagne, to find the unit deserted. The note telling him that he was a bastard and that Hannah never wanted to see him again had been enough of a shock for him to be still feeling stunned when he'd taken the second call from his ex-mother-in-law, Cheryl, informing him of the existence of his son.

He'd never discovered exactly what Cheryl had said to Hannah when she had taken the first phone call but it had clearly been enough for her to assume he'd still been married and had a family. Hannah had never given Jack the courtesy of permission to offer an explanation. She had already packed her bags and left for the airport by the time he'd tried the door of her unit. The letters he'd sent to her new department in Auckland weeks later, when life had calmed down enough to allow time, had been returned. Unopened.

It would never have worked in any case. Hannah hadn't felt anything like the same way he had. Getting married and having a child so soon after their fling had proved that. And she was cold. Anyone who could dump someone so emphatically and unilaterally had to be hard-hearted. Even now, years later, she wasn't prepared to be remotely friendly or to consider the possibility that her judgement might have been misplaced. Hannah Campbell was quite prepared to act as judge and jury on unchallenged evidence. What's more, she was equally prepared to execute the punishment and it appeared his sentence was by no means complete. Fate may have brought them together for a third time but the only lucky outcome would be to get past any effect she was capable of generating in his body *or* mind.

Enough was enough.

By the time Jack headed to the ward to check on the

post-operative condition of Daniel Chubb, his former irritation with Hannah's attitude had been augmented by
the unwelcome memories to become a full-blown resentment that rivalled the feelings he had experienced
when his marriage had gone down the tubes over seven
years ago. Daniel was fine, already bouncing back from
the surgery with the kind of ability many babies had.
His vital signs were all normal and he was already feeding again happily. The parents were grateful and easily
reassured that the small amount of bowel that had been
removed would have no long-term effects on Daniel's
intestinal function.

'All he's going to have to show for this is a very small
scar. And maybe his hospital bracelet, if you have a
scrapbook to stick it in.'

'I've been meaning to start one.' Daniel's mother
smiled. 'I think I'll do that as soon as we get home.
How long will that be?'

'Only a day or two. I'll come back and see how Daniel
is in the morning.'

Jack paused in the ward office to scribble a record of
his visit and chart some pain relief for Daniel if it became necessary later. He really ought to do something
about the scrapbook he'd often thought of making for
Ben. He had more than one hospital bracelet in that
shoebox of mementoes. Trouble was, there were chunks
of his son's history that were far easier to bury than
confront. Just like his own. If he couldn't do it for himself, how would he help Ben when he got old enough
to start asking difficult questions?

As he left the ward, Jack looked up to see Hannah
entering her office and he knew he couldn't let this situation go any further. The way Hannah had treated him
five years ago had been unfair. To continue treating him

like this when he was trying to start a new and better life for both himself and his son was simply malicious. Jack rapped on the half-open door of Hannah's office, stepped inside without waiting for a response and closed the door behind him.

The intrusion was startling. It became slightly alarming as the door swung shut, enclosing Hannah in a space that was far too small when it was being shared with Jack Douglas. His size was enough to be almost intimidating at close quarters anyway. Coupled with the grimly determined expression enhancing the strong lines of his face, his presence in her office was vaguely threatening. Damn it, this was *her* office. *Her* space. And she hadn't issued any invitation for Jack to enter. The retreat into annoyance must have been obvious because Jack's half-smile lacked any kind of warmth.

'I get the distinct impression you're not happy to see me, Hannah.'

'I'm rather busy.'

'I won't take up much of your time.' Jack leaned on the back of the chair positioned in front of Hannah's desk. 'And I wasn't referring to this precise moment. You seem to have embarked on a campaign designed to make it obvious that you're not happy having to work with me.'

Hannah merely raised her eyebrows. She wasn't about to admit to an unprofessional personal vendetta, and she hadn't embarked on one in any case. All she had done had been to maintain a personal distance and make damned sure that any professional interaction had been faultless on her part. She could hardly be blamed for being immune to the charm Jack Douglas was using to gain such instant popularity amongst the majority of other staff members.

'I have nothing against you professionally, Jack. I've been hearing a lot about you from Peter Smiley and others. I understand your CV is very impressive.'

'Ditto.' The smile was more genuine now but Jack's gaze was still very direct. 'I also understand that you are applying for a paediatric consultancy in this hospital.'

'Yes. I am.' Hannah resisted the impulse to look away. Or maybe she was trying to summon one. Jack's dark eyes had lost nothing of the compelling quality she remembered.

'Then it's highly likely we'll be working together at regular intervals for quite some time. If you get the job.'

'I suppose it is.' Hannah frowned as she tried to glean any hidden message in Jack's words. What else had he heard from the talkative head of her department? Was someone else rumoured to have a better chance of winning the position? Or was Jack implying that her unwelcoming reception for a new surgeon might have been noted and counted against her? She stared at Jack, trying to remember whether her deliberate coolness had really broken any boundaries of acceptable behaviour between colleagues.

'I have no intention of moving elsewhere.' Jack hesitated for a moment and then ran his tongue over his lower lip before continuing. 'Whatever happened between us in the past should not be allowed to have a bearing on establishing or maintaining a professional relationship.'

Hannah had unconsciously mirrored his action and moistened her own lips. Then she caught her lower lip between her teeth firmly enough to be painful. Good grief! The memories of physical touch from this man were hard enough to handle and here she was experiencing a surge of what could only be a reawakened desire brought on by nothing more than a glimpse of his tongue on his lip. Hannah jerked her gaze away from his face only to find her line of vision caught by the hands gripping the back of the spare chair. Large, capable hands with a surgeon's long fingers. Hands and fingers that were capable of... With another jerk, Hannah transferred her gaze to the patch of desk directly in front of her. She picked up a ballpoint pen and idly clicked it on.

'Whatever happened between us is history, Jack. Long gone.' Pushing the side of the pen released the spring with another satisfying click. 'And long forgotten,' she added firmly.

'Ditto,' Jack said again.

Hannah pushed the end of the pen inwards again. 'I'm sorry if I've made you feel unwelcome but I think I made it fairly clear how I felt before I left Auckland.'

'You mean the bit about never wanting to see or speak to me again?'

The tiny silence hung between them until Hannah snorted softly. 'Not entirely forgotten, then.'

'Some things *are* difficult to forget. Or forgive.'

'I couldn't agree more.' Hannah's direct stare was deliberate but Jack wasn't going to acknowledge the accusation.

'Like your lack of interest in any explanation I might have been able to offer.'

Hannah shook her head with disbelief. Did Jack really think that an 'explanation' would have excused the fact he'd lied about having a wife and child? She knew what the explanation would have been. He was separated. Or divorced. Just like Paul had been before him. No strings.

Nothing to stop him falling in love again. Of living with her even, and planning a future. Of letting her build her life around him...until he decided that perhaps it was time to try again with his original choice for a partner. Bitter memories came in layers sometimes. Like an onion. And peeling any more of them away would only make her cry.

'It wouldn't have made any difference, Jack.'

'No. I don't suppose it would have.' Jack held Hannah's stare then looked away and sighed wearily. 'You don't give anyone much of a chance, do you, Hannah Campbell?'

'I gave you far too much of a chance, Jack. I won't be making that mistake again, thanks.'

'You'll be pleased to know I won't be asking.' Jack met her gaze again only fleetingly. 'I don't like people with closed minds.'

'And I don't like people who can't be trusted.'

The silence lasted longer this time. It had a defeated feel to it as though something had been lost. By both of them.

'It doesn't sound like a very good basis for professional compatibility, does it?'

'I'm sure we're both adult enough to deal with it.'

'Let's hope so.'

The summons to the emergency department within seconds of leaving Hannah's office was a diversion Jack was grateful to receive. A child had fallen through a plate-glass window and some of the abdominal lacerations were deep enough to require the attention of a surgeon. At least this was something Jack knew he could deal with. As far as the situation with Hannah went, he wasn't sure he had achieved anything at all by that encounter. He'd even had the uncomfortable impression that he had been expected to make some form of apology when it was Hannah's behaviour that was and always had been far more unacceptable. OK, so he hadn't told her the whole story of his life in the first few hours they'd had together but he hadn't lied and he'd been perfectly sincere about the depth of his attraction to her. Even now, he had been prepared to forgive and forget. To move on and establish a new relationship of some kind.

What he wasn't prepared to do was accept Hannah's narrow-minded judgement of his character as being justified in any way. And he wasn't going to apologise.

Damn it. He had nothing to apologise *for*.

CHAPTER FOUR

THE nerve of the man!

When the door had closed behind Jack on his way out of her office, Hannah found herself simply staring at it for a full five minutes, having been left with the impression that he actually believed that the major cause of any animosity between them could be laid at *her* feet.

OK, so maybe he couldn't have known just how deep a nerve his deception had struck at the time, but at least *she* had been completely honest about the emotional attachments in her life. He also couldn't know how the repercussions of their time together had affected her life. Hannah had already accepted that she couldn't blame Jack for the unopened return of the letter she'd written to inform him of her pregnancy but how could she have known that he hadn't taken up the position he'd been offered at the National Children's Hospital? Hannah had turned down her own offer of the senior registrar's post well before she'd discovered her impending motherhood because the prospect of working in the same hospital as Jack had been unthinkable. Had he felt the same way?

It had only been a one-night stand, for heaven's sake. How on earth did it still have the ability to stir up such an intense emotional response? Hannah knew why. She had never had what could be considered a one-night stand. If there hadn't been something extraordinary between herself and Jack she would never have stayed with him that night. She wouldn't have experienced anything like the grief that overseas phone call had generated and she wouldn't have spent months—no…years—haunted by the aftermath of that brief union.

It wasn't that she had a closed mind. Far from it. Hannah had explored every possibility that might have let Jack off the hook a million times but there had been no way to avoid the bottom line. A wife, especially if estranged, was one thing. A child was something completely different. Hannah knew intimately now what kind of bond that created and for Jack to have denied it so convincingly meant that either he was an expert liar or, worse, he felt no bond with his child. And that would mean her judgement of his whole personality had been horribly wrong.

Either way, the blame lay with Jack, so how could he possibly think he could waltz into her life and expect a warm welcome? He clearly didn't have any inkling that an apology of some kind might be in order and he'd had the nerve to suggest that her interaction with him on a professional front might sway her chances of winning that consultancy. Not only had he gained a permanent position in *her* hospital, he was now almost issuing a warning that she'd better accept him as a colleague if she wanted to earn the same status.

And maybe she did. Hannah groaned aloud as she took the weight of her forehead in the palm of her hand. She *had* been rude to Jack. Attack had seemed the best form of defence and she had felt an overwhelming need to defend herself. The shock of finding how lightly buried her memories of Jack were had been augmented by the total failure over the last ten days to prevent herself cataloguing the features her daughter might have inherited from her father.

The deep brown eyes. The curls. The laughter that was always so close to the surface. Even the *niceness*. The desire to give and the genuine ability to gain as much pleasure as the recipient of her offerings. That had been the impression of Jack that had been impossible to expunge completely and that was why his betrayal had been so unbelievably hurtful.

Thinking of Olivia was enough to make Hannah move. It was only just 4 p.m. but she had caught up with all her patients, including young Daniel Chubb, who was doing very well after his surgery. She would escape early and spend time with her daughter. She would use that time to remind herself just what was important in her life. Why this consultancy was so pivotal to her future and why it was imperative that she let go of the past and find a way to work with Jack in a civilised manner.

The real bottom line was that she had a lot to thank Jack for because if it hadn't been for him then Olivia would not exist. Having a child might have slowed her career progression, made things far more difficult financially and altered the whole focus of her life dramatically, but Hannah couldn't imagine being without her now. She was the centre of Hannah's life and gave her hope for the future she would never have otherwise had. She had someone to love who would not betray her as all the significant men in her life had. Perhaps Jack had done her a favour, in fact. At least Hannah wouldn't end up like her own mother, raising her children and living with the knowledge she could never trust their father to remain faithful.

Arriving at Maysfield Child Care by 4.30 p.m. was a treat and Hannah's spirits lifted immeasurably. She could cope with working with Jack. She would get used to it eventually and start to feel safe again. One of these days she would be able to look back on this period as just being a temporary hassle. The kind that sorted itself

out as so many others had done over the years she had
managed alone.

Like the worry she'd had about child care when Olivia
started school in just a few months. The babysitter
Hannah could use at nights and weekends was the sev-
enteen-year-old daughter of her closest neighbour, the
farmer she leased Joseph's paddock from. Emma was as
much a vital part of her support system as the Maysfield
Child Care Centre but it would have been impossible for
her to care for Olivia on school days. With the new
service being offered by the centre, that worry had evaporated. She could continue to transfer her daughter's care
to Shirley and her staff at 7 a.m., knowing that Olivia
would be taken to school and then collected by people
she could trust absolutely. It wasn't ideal, of course—
Hannah would much rather be doing it herself. But as
far as a compromise went, it was perfect.

Other parents clearly thought so as well. The new service had only been in place for a week but an extra half-
dozen children had expanded the centre's regular clients
already. If any of the parents or staff had been concerned
by the potential change in dynamics of adding older children to the social mix, they had probably had the same
pleasant surprise Hannah had experienced so far. Four
of the newcomers were older siblings of children already
using the centre. The other two, a six-year-old girl and
a seven-year-old boy, had fitted in so comfortably it was
already hard to imagine the place without them.

Hannah was smiling as she walked alongside the
wrought-iron railings separating the car-parking area
from the large garden of the converted villa. Given the
lovely weather, she should have guessed that Olivia
would be sitting in her favourite spot, tucked into the
hollow of the overgrown japonica shrub, with a fat, con-

tented rabbit filling her lap. Hannah was also unsurprised to see the curly dark head of her companion almost touching Olivia's blond curls as her new friend leaned forward to post the end of a long blade of grass into the rabbit's co-operative mouth.

The friendship between these two children had been instantaneous. Apparently, Olivia had gone straight to the boy as he'd stepped from the van, having been collected from school for the first time. He'd been standing beside Shirley, clutching his school backpack and sizing up the unfamiliar environment when Olivia had simply appeared and taken hold of his hand.

'Come on,' she had ordered. 'I'll show you Bugs. He's our rabbit and he's really *fat*.'

Bugs was probably even fatter now, thanks to the children's delight in watching the food disappearing with such consistent appreciation.

'I'm getting a bit worried about Bugs,' Hannah told Shirley after greeting her. 'He's going to develop a major weight problem at this rate.'

'I'll put him on a diet next week.' Shirley smiled. 'I just haven't had the heart to interfere with the bonding process he's provided.'

'Hmm.' Hannah was staring from the window into the garden now. Most of the children still in the centre were listening to Suzanna reading a story. A few were still playing in the sandpit under Lucy's watchful gaze, but Olivia and her friend were totally focused on the rabbit. 'I don't think she's even noticed I'm here yet. Do you know, she didn't even want to come home straight away on Tuesday? She wanted to stay and play with Ben.'

Shirley nodded. 'As soon as the van leaves to do the after school pick-up run, she goes and sits near the gate, watching for it to come back. It was love at first sight for those two. It's so cute.'

'Is it normal for children to form such intense friendships so quickly? Seems like I've heard nothing but "Ben said…" or "Ben and I did…" all week.'

'Olivia's a very loving little girl. Something about Ben obviously appealed the moment she set eyes on him.'

'But he's so much older than she is. I wouldn't have thought a seven-year-old boy would have the slightest interest in playing with her.'

Shirley just smiled. 'Ben's a neat kid. He's not your average little boy. I think he's quite sensitive. And gentle. Olivia made him feel a part of the place from the moment he got here and now he feels important because she's so keen to see him.'

'Do they play with other children as well?' Hannah frowned. What if Ben's parents decided to change their child care arrangements and the boy vanished from Olivia's orbit just as suddenly as he had appeared? 'She never mentions Jane or Lydia or Adam these days. She didn't even want to watch her video last night because she was too busy making a card for Ben. She was worried he might be sick.'

'He doesn't come on Wednesdays or Fridays. Maybe we didn't explain that well enough. She showed us the card at news time this morning. She did put a lot of effort into it, didn't she?'

'I think she used up our whole supply of glitter and glue.' Hannah grinned. 'Bet you've never seen a donkey that sparkled like that.'

Both women were silent for a moment as they gazed from the window. Olivia had finally noticed her mother's arrival. Her face lit up and she waved happily but instead of leaping to her feet she turned back to Ben and the conversation appeared to become quite animated.

'Actually, I've been wanting to have a quiet word to you about Ben Sullivan.'

Something in Shirley's tone made Hannah turn sharply back towards the older woman.

'I only noticed today. I guess it's because it's so much warmer and he's wearing shorts.' Shirley's brow creased. 'It's probably nothing, but he does seem to have rather a lot of bruises on his legs. I just wanted to ask your professional opinion on whether it was something I should follow up. I've never had to even think about what to do if I became involved in a case of child abuse, but it's not something I can afford to be complacent about.'

'I certainly wouldn't jump to any conclusions,' Hannah cautioned. 'Some children do bruise more easily than others. Look at Livvy. She's managed to look positively battered at times, the way bruises show up on her pale skin. And legs are pretty common places to collect marks. Especially with small boys who might be a bit more adventurous on climbing equipment or play rougher games like rugby.' But Hannah frowned slightly herself. Was Ben spending his time with her daughter because he was being badly treated by children his own age at school? Or, worse, being badly treated at home? 'Are the bruises just on his legs?'

'I noticed some odd marks on his arm earlier. He had his sleeves rolled up when he and Livvy were floating boats in the water tray before they went to feed Bugs. I wouldn't know about anywhere else.'

'Does his behaviour seem at all unusual to you? Is he more withdrawn than you might expect? Or nervous?'

'No.' Shirley shook her head more firmly this time.

'As I said, he's neat. Quiet, certainly, but he seems perfectly happy. Quite mature for his age, really.'

'Have you met his parents?'

'No. Suzanna did the enrolment, which was initiated through the school. We've got a copy of his birth certificate but the school hasn't forwarded any other records yet. It's his nanny that collects him. In fact, that's her arriving now. The one talking on her mobile near the gate.'

The story was finished and children started moving purposefully towards new activities in the large room. Another parent arrived who wanted a word with Shirley so Hannah went to the cloakroom to collect Olivia's backpack, her blue jacket and the soft toy dog she had left lying on the floor beneath her peg. When she went outside she found that Bugs had been put back into the run attached to his hutch.

'Mummy! Can Ben come home with us and play at my house?'

'I can't see why not, darling. If Ben wants to, that is.'

'He wants to, Mummy. Can he come today?'

'No, not today, sweetheart.'

'Please?'

'It's not the sort of thing we can do just like that, Livvy. We'd need to make arrangements.'

'But he doesn't believe we've got a donkey.'

'Don't you, Ben?' Hannah smiled at the boy standing beside the rabbit's hutch. Solemn brown eyes gazed back at her.

'I've never seen a donkey,' he said. 'Livvy says I can have a ride on him.'

'And he wants to see the alphabet hens.'

'I'm sure he can…one day.' Hannah was still smiling at Ben. His accent suggested he was new to the country as well as Maysfield Child Care. He was small for his age, but there was something about the dark eyes and riot of matching curls that was very appealing. And then Ben smiled back at her and she could see why Olivia was so enchanted with his company.

'Today?' Olivia tugged at Hannah's hand. 'Please, Mummy. I really, really want to take Ben home with us.'

Hannah was relieved to notice the swift approach of Ben's nanny. She wouldn't have to be the bad guy and refuse her daughter's pleas alone.

'Come on, Ben. We've got to hurry. I've got an essay I've got to get finished, 'cos I'm going out later tonight.'

Hannah wasn't surprised that Ben's face fell. It was hardly a greeting intended to make a small boy feel wanted. She looked away from the sad little face and it was then that Hannah noticed the marks on Ben's forearm. A pattern of slender bruises that sent a chill down Hannah's spine. Maybe Shirley had done the right thing in requesting a professional opinion. Hannah had seen marks like that. They looked very like the kind of bruises you could expect when adult fingers gripped a small arm far too tightly.

'Ben wants to come and play at my house,' Olivia informed the young woman.

'Can I, Lisa?'

'I dunno about that.' Lisa looked taken aback.

'You wouldn't have to look after me,' Ben pointed out. 'You could do your homework.'

Lisa looked at Hannah. 'Are you her mum?'

Hannah nodded. Lisa didn't look much older than Emma. She also looked stressed. Did she have the experience or the patience to be a caregiver for a young child?

'I have this paper I was supposed to hand in at varsity today,' Lisa told Hannah. 'I just haven't been able to find the time and I'm going to be in so much trouble if it's not done by tomorrow. An hour or two would be a real godsend.'

'I'm quite happy to have Ben come and visit,' Hannah said slowly. 'As long as it's all right with his parents.' If Olivia was so friendly with Ben, maybe she had an excuse to try a casual approach to find out whether there was anything unacceptable about the boy's home life. Hannah was looking at the collection of bruises on Ben's legs now. One or two of them looked quite nasty. It was all too easy for people to ignore the unpleasant possibilities often covered by an 'accident prone' label for a child. Maybe Hannah had a responsibility to become involved now that this had been brought to her attention. Ben did seem undersized for his age. And he also appeared quite happy to postpone going home for a while.

'I can give you my address and phone number,' Hannah told Lisa as they followed Ben towards the cloakroom. 'If there's any problem with collecting Ben from our place, I'll be quite happy to drive him home later. I'm a doctor,' she added. 'And the staff here have known me for years if you need any reassurance.'

'Oh, no. I'm sure it'll be fine.' Lisa handed Ben his jacket and backpack. 'I'll leave a message and his dad can come and get him on his way home from work. It might not be till about 6 p.m., though.'

'No problem. Ben can have something to eat with Livvy.' Hannah was scribbling her details onto a scrap of paper. Shirley caught her gaze as she handed the paper to Lisa.

'Ben's coming to play for a while at our house,' she explained. 'He wants to meet Joseph.'

The message Hannah received in response was clear. A period of informal observation could well be enough to let Hannah know whether Shirley had any grounds to follow up her concerns, and who better to make those observations and possibily initiate an investigation than a qualified paediatrician?

It felt odd, taking two children home with her. Hannah had never felt the need to encourage Olivia to develop friendships that extended into home life. Her daughter got all the social interaction she needed during her time at day care and the hours for just the two of them were too precious to share. It came as somewhat of a revelation to discover that the company Ben provided made her time with Olivia even more enjoyable. It was delightful to hear her daughter chattering non-stop, laughing so often and being so determined that her guest should enjoy himself as much as she did. Hannah was proud that Olivia was so generous and eager to share the things she loved.

'These are *my* gumboots. They're pink, see?'

'I don't have any gumboots,' Ben said sadly.

'You can have one of mine,' Olivia offered promptly. 'And we could both hop. Like this.' She hopped for three steps before collapsing in giggles.

'I don't think Ben would want to wear pink gumboots.' Hannah smiled. 'Besides, his feet are a bit bigger than yours.'

'But he'll get his shoes muddy.' Olivia's eyes widened with concern. 'And then he might get into trouble!'

'Nah. I can get muddy shoes if I want,' Ben informed her loftily. 'Dad doesn't mind.'

Hannah absorbed the statement as she went to the shed to find the old pair of rubber overshoes she used for gardening. No hint there of any parental reaction to be feared. And Shirley had been right in her impression of Ben's gentle nature. Hannah had watched him greet the cats when they had arrived home and his touch had been careful enough to have both pets clamouring for more.

'I like Sooty best,' Ben had decided.

'That's Snow.'

'No, it's not. He's black.'

Hannah had had to explain. 'Livvy was only two when we got the kittens and she got the names mixed up for so long they kind of stuck. Snow's the black cat and Sooty's the white one.'

Ben had thought about that for a few seconds as he'd continued stroking the black cat. 'I like Snow best,' he amended. Then he caught Hannah's gaze and grinned. And she grinned right back, amazed that a child could appreciate the humour and impressed that he would de-cide to participate instead of belittling the private joke. She liked this boy a lot.

So did the cats. Sooty and Snow followed them as far as the henhouse, where Olivia showed Ben where to grab handfuls of wheat to scatter.

'Deirdre's hatched her eggs, see?' Olivia's face split into a huge grin as she caught sight of the newly hatched chicks coming towards them. 'That's Fred in the front.'

'How do you know it's a boy?' Ben queried.

'We don't,' Hannah said. 'We'll just have to wait and see.'

'What are the other chickens called?'

'Gina and Harriet and Inky.'

Ben looked impressed. 'Are you going to have the whole alphabet one day?'

'I'm not sure about that.' Hannah managed to ignore

Olivia's enthusiastic nodding. 'Twenty-six hens would be rather a lot.'

'Are we going to let Ben have a ride on Joseph?' Olivia wiped small dusty hands on the legs of her dungarees.

'Sure, if that's what Ben would like to do.'

If Hannah had had any doubts about how likable Ben was, they vanished completely over the next hour as she led her patient, long-eared pet on circuits of the orchard. She had no qualms about letting Ben try the last round by himself and the sheer joy on his face as he rode back toward them was contagious. Joseph even obliged by producing a sedate trot on the homeward leg and Ben was so proud of himself.

'I can ride,' he told Olivia. 'Did you see how fast I went?'

'You didn't even fall off.' Olivia's blue eyes shone with admiration.

'Can I do it again, Hannah? Please?'

'Next time,' Hannah promised. 'We'd better take Joe's saddle and bridle off now and give him a rest. It's nearly six o'clock so we'd better get back to the house in case your dad comes to get you. He might not find us out here. Besides, aren't you hungry?'

The phone was ringing as they approached the house but it had stopped by the time the trio piled into the kitchen and Hannah forgot to check for any messages. The children were hungry, not to mention grubby and tired and happy. Hannah decided they needed a quick meal so she turned on the toasted-sandwichmaker and sliced some fresh bread.

'What shall we put in our toasties? Cheese?'

'Worms!' Olivia shouted gleefully.

Hannah tried to look stern. 'Spaghetti,' she corrected firmly. 'What would you like, Ben?'

'Spaghetti, please. *And* cheese.'

Hannah was pulling the can from the pantry when she heard him whispering something to Olivia. 'Worms' was the only clear word she caught, but the sound of their shared mirth was enough to make her pretend she hadn't heard a thing.

'Better wash your hands, guys,' she instructed. 'We'll have the toasties and then it'll be time to get you home, Ben.' The glance at her watch was disturbing. It was well after 6 p.m. now and there was no sign of a parent arriving for Ben. She had given Lisa all her details. Why hadn't it occurred to her to get the same in return? At least Ben was old enough to know his own address and phone number.

Except he wasn't.

'I don't know the name of our street. We've just moved there. It's number fourteen, though. Flat three.'

'Have you got a telephone?'

'Course we have.'

'Do you know the number?'

'It's got two threes in it.'

'Cool.' Hannah smiled. ' Don't worry about it. I'll figure something out. You finish your toasties and I'll make some hot chocolate in a minute.' Hannah went into the hall where the children had abandoned their backpacks. Any responsible parent would have ensured that Ben's name and contact details were written somewhere on his belongings.

It was nowhere obvious. Hannah pulled out reading books, a large folded piece of artwork and an oversized lunchbox to check whether there was a label inside Ben's backpack. She was still holding the lunchbox as the sound of footsteps on her verandah heralded some-one's rapid approach. The strength of the rap on the door was disconcerting enough to make her drop the lunchbox as she straightened hurriedly. Whoever was knocking did not sound particularly happy.

The man standing on her verandah looked even less happy than the knock had suggested. He looked posi-tively furious. Hannah's jaw dropped.

'What the hell are *you* doing here?''

'What I'd like to know,' Jack countered icily,' 'is what the hell my son is doing *here*?'

Fight or flight.

Some detached portion of Hannah's brain noted her physical reaction to the lash of fear. Her mouth went dry, her heart pounded and her stomach clenched. The danger that having Jack on her home territory repre-sented was huge. What if he saw Olivia? What if he guessed she was older than Hannah had claimed? Or, worse, if he recognised some genetic bond that would make it impossible to hide the truth?

Yes, flight was tempting but the impulse to slam the door in Jack's face and run was simply not feasible. If only she had known that it was his son she had taken home with them that afternoon. Why the different sur-name? It felt like a new deception had wrapped her in sticky tentacles and any resolve Hannah might have had to start being civil to this man went straight out the win-dow. No. Flight was not the answer and Hannah mus-tered her resources to fight with no more than a barely discernible hesitation. The children were safely tucked away in the kitchen at the other end of the hallway but Hannah kept her voice down just in case.

'You were supposed to collect Ben at 6 p.m. Do you have any idea what the time is right now?'

'Nearly 7.' A muscle in Jack's jaw tightened noticeably. 'If you knew I was coming to collect Ben, why couldn't you have had the decency to call and let me know precisely where he was? And with whom?'

'I didn't know *you* were coming to collect him. I was expecting his father. A Mr Sullivan, strangely enough.'

'I *am* Ben's father.'

'If I'd known that, I wouldn't have brought him home in the first place.'

'You're lucky you don't have the police on your doorstep right now.'

'Excuse me?'

'I arrived home an hour ago expecting to find my son and his nanny. What I found was an empty house and no indication of their whereabouts.'

Hannah pushed away the sympathy she could so easily summon. What if she came home to find Emma and Olivia missing unexpectedly? The automatic assumption would be that some disaster had occurred. That her child might be being searched for or being rushed to hospital after an accident. But this wasn't her fault and Jack had no right to direct his anger towards her. 'Lisa said she'd leave you a message. I wrote down my address and phone number for her.'

'I didn't realise the potential significance of that scrap of paper until I'd spent half an hour trying to track Lisa down. I tried ringing the number and got no answer. I finally rang that irresponsible woman who runs the day care centre and she told me where I could find Ben.'

'Shirley Smith is *not* irresponsible.' Hannah felt far more angry than frightened now. 'She is one of the most caring and qualified people you could be fortunate enough to find for child care, and *I* should know. She's been a second mother to my daughter for years.'

'I'll be making other arrangements for Ben in future. I think my standards of care might be set a little higher than yours, Dr Campbell.'

'Oh, really?' Hannah's tone was scathing. 'That's not the impression I got.'

'What the hell is that supposed to mean?'

Hannah was about to win this confrontation. Any warning bells about using the ace up her sleeve were easy to ignore. The possibility of being even more a threat to Jack than he was to her was too good a form of defence to resist.

'Ben's physical condition is a little too obvious to ignore,' Hannah said quietly. 'You might find that your ''standards of care'' need some adjustment.'

Jack's mouth opened and then closed again, with no words coming out.

'If my daughter had bruising anything like Ben's, I'd be more than a little concerned,' Hannah continued relentlessly. Her confidence was increasing steadily. 'Unless, of course, there's a reasonable explanation.'

She could almost see Jack collecting his anger. Reining it in. Withdrawing. His face became virtually expressionless. 'I doubt that you would be remotely interested in any explanation I might have to offer.' The words held a wealth of bitterness. 'And so I'm not about to provide one. Not to you, anyway. This is none of your business.'

'I have no desire to become involved in your personal life.' Hannah could hear the noise level in the kitchen rising. If she moved quickly, perhaps she could extract Ben without Olivia having to come anywhere near Jack. 'For Ben's sake, however, I hope you can sort it out before someone else makes it *their* business. I'm not the only one who's noticed.'

'I'm sure you're the only one who's jumped to conclusions.' Hannah wouldn't have thought it possible for such warm brown eyes to project such a chilling coldness. 'I can't believe I was ever misguided enough to fall in love with you, Hannah Campbell.'

The silence that followed Jack's words was enough for the proverbial pin dropping to have sounded loud. It lasted only a split second, however, before being shattered by a young and very excited voice.

'Dad!' Ben was racing down the hallway, with Olivia in hot pursuit. Hannah had to step back and open the door wider to prevent a collision.

'Whoa! Take it easy, mate.' Jack caught his son and put an arm around his skinny shoulders. 'Sorry I'm late, Ben. I had no idea where you were.'

'I've been riding Joseph, Dad. He's a donkey! And we've fed the alphabet hens and Livvy's got cats and Snow's black and there's this cool hedge outside. We're going to build a hut in it next time I come.'

Jack's gaze grazed Hannah's face for just long enough to relay the message that there would be no 'next time'.

'Let's go, buddy. We'll get a hamburger for dinner on the way home, yes?'

'I've had tea.' Ben wiped some more of the tomato sauce from his face.

Olivia poked her head out from behind Hannah's legs. 'We had worms,' she said gravely. 'Inside toasties.'

'Where's your bag, Ben?' Jack barely glanced at Olivia. 'What's all that stuff doing on the floor?''

'I didn't do it,' Ben protested.

'Sorry, Ben. I was looking to see if you had your address and phone number inside.'

'Inside his lunchbox?' Jack's words were not soft enough to disguise his distaste. 'Or were you looking for something else? Sorry to disappoint you but Ben is not neglected as far as his diet is concerned.' He raised his voice again. 'Don't forget your shoes, mate.'

'I'll get them.' Olivia pounced on the sneakers lying by the kitchen door. 'They haven't got *any* mud on them,' she informed Jack proudly.

The expected appreciation was not forthcoming and Hannah saw the confusion growing in Olivia's eyes. She hadn't heard any of the unpleasant exchange between the adults but some level of understanding that Ben's father was not happy about this visit was clearly filtering through. She took Hannah's hand and held it tightly, pulling her mother as she trailed after Ben towards their car.

'What have you got to say to Hannah, Ben?'

'Thank you for having me,' Ben said politely.

'It was a pleasure,' Hannah said warmly. 'We had fun, didn't we?'

'Me, too,' Olivia piped. 'I had *lots* of fun.' She turned an earnest face towards Jack. 'I love Ben,' she announced. 'He's my friend.'

Jack caught Hannah's gaze once more. 'Nice kid,' he murmured. 'Takes after her father, does she?'

CHAPTER FIVE

THE irony of the insult was haunting.

The space of more than a week had afforded plenty of time for Hannah to recognise just how out of control her emotions had been. She had exacerbated, if not created, a problem that she should, and could, have taken in her stride. Fear that Jack would somehow recognise his daughter and demand access had faded as abruptly as Ben had been removed from her house that evening. It hadn't happened and it was unlikely that Jack would ever get that close to Olivia again. He wanted as little as possible to do with Hannah now. He was treating her with precisely the same professional coolness, albeit minus the faint condescension, that she had embraced to deal with him.

And Hannah didn't like it.

All she had received now as Jack and Barry had passed her in the ward corridor had been a nod, acknowledging her presence. Then Jack leaned on the sill of the window into the ward clerk's office, a warm smile softening his stern expression.

'Annie, how are you? How was your weekend?'

'Jack!' Anne's tone conveyed her pleasure in seeing the surgeon. 'What a nice way to start my Monday morning. My weekend was great. How was yours?'

'Brilliant. I took Ben to Orana Park. They've got a new batch of baby lions in the nursery. He loved it.'

Hannah pulled the set of notes she had been searching for from the trolley. Olivia would have loved a trip to the wildlife park as well. Especially if it had been in Ben's company. The relief of finding that Jack hadn't followed through on his threat to change the after-school care arrangements for his son last week had been undermined by Olivia's persistent requests for Ben to come and visit again. Hannah knew it wasn't going to happen. Ben also seemed to know and had accepted what he couldn't change philosophically.

'Dad was a bit cross,' he'd told Hannah by way of explanation. 'He said I shouldn't have gone riding when I wasn't wearing a crash helmet.'

'I wouldn't have let you do anything dangerous without a helmet on, Ben.'

'I know.' Ben's smile was curiously adult. 'Dad just worries about me.'

'Fair enough.' It hadn't been the first prod to Hannah's conscience over her reference to Ben's bruises and it wouldn't be the last, but the reaction from Jack also smacked of finding an excuse to keep Ben apart from Olivia. Joseph was a tiny donkey, for goodness' sake. Ben's feet hadn't been far off the ground and the long grass in the orchard would have cushioned any tumble perfectly well. It wasn't as though she'd put the kid on a feisty pony and sent him cross-country.

Jack finished his socialising with the ward staff as Hannah pulled the last set of notes she needed from the wheeled rack. She moved away as Jack approached but was then forced to pause.

'Excuse me, Hannah, but do you have Stella Petersen's notes there?'

'Yes, I do. I'm just on my way to see her. We'll be starting our ward round as soon as Peter arrives.'

'Perhaps I could borrow them for the moment. She's first on my list as well.'

'Of course.' Hannah handed over the notes. 'Have you reconsidered last week's decision about further surgery, then?' It wasn't just that she was talking to Jack that made Hannah's tone so subdued. Stella Petersen was a three-year-old girl who had first presented with a highly malignant genito-urinary tract tumour six months ago. Chemotherapy, surgery and radiation had slowed but sadly not halted the progress of the disease. Hannah hadn't been surprised when the oncology team had decided to call on Jack's expertise. The training and experience he'd had in paediatric surgery specifically associated with cancers had stood out in the copy of the CV she had seen. Not that anyone was expecting miracles now. Any more surgery was likely to be considered only for palliative reasons.

'I'll be discussing that with Peter after I've seen her. I expect we'll be having a family conference later on this morning.'

The inference was that Hannah would not be required to take part in the discussion process. Exclusion would be unreasonable given the input Hannah had already had in Stella's treatment over the months and the relationship she had forged with the family, but Hannah made no comment. There was little she could do to modify the way Jack was acting towards her other than to retain control of her own behaviour and wait for an opportunity to make some form of apology.

The only real threat Jack presented now was the possibility of him discussing her on a personal level with his fellow surgical consultant, who would be a member of the panel conducting the appointment interviews next week. A casual hint concerning her unsuitability due to her perceived lack of judgement might be all that was needed to tip the balance, and why wouldn't he take such an opportunity? She had, after all, practically accused him of physically abusing his own son, and anyone who had seen Jack interacting with one of his young patients would know how ridiculous an accusation that was.

More than once now Hannah had been present when Jack had examined one of her patients, and she found herself close to tears this morning at the exquisitely gentle touch he had for Stella Petersen. The tiny girl's tumour was now the biggest part of her and even the continuous morphine infusion couldn't prevent her pain on being handled in any way. Somehow Jack managed without causing more than a whimper and when he finished with the grossly distended abdomen he stroked the child's cheek with his thumb and smiled at her. Miraculously, Stella smiled back and that was when Hannah almost choked on the lump in her throat.

Jack had touched her once, in exactly the same manner. A gentle stroke with the ball of his thumb down the side of her cheek and along her jaw. Seeing Stella's smile had brought back so vividly the tenderness of the gesture and the way it had made her feel so cherished. She hoped Stella felt something like that. As though she was the only person in the world who really mattered. It wasn't much to offer but there was precious little more the medical team could do for her now.

The family conference was used to gather the support team that would allow Stella's parents to take her home to die with as little discomfort as possible. There was no real need for a surgeon to be present but Jack was there, along with Peter and Hannah and William. An oncology consultant was also there, along with the paediatric outreach nursing team. A counsellor and chaplain took the numbers in the room to such that Hannah could sit quietly and inconspicuously as she struggled more than usual to cope with a tragic outcome for a small patient she had come to love.

Hannah was due in the neonatal intensive care unit after the conference finished but she couldn't tear herself away from the ward just yet. Stella's final discharge proved to be an emotionally draining experience for everyone involved. Hannah watched the small girl being carried away in her father's arms and the hug and tears she shared with Stella's mother did little to ease her own distress. Hannah waited until the lift door closed on the Petersen family and their support team and then she turned and walked to the window that looked down onto the greenery of the park as she searched for composure.

Hearing Jack speak to Stella's parents had been one of the hardest aspects of the whole discharge procedure. There could have been no denying the genuine empathy in his tone—the sadness that his team could contribute nothing more. Jack could no more set out to hurt a child than Hannah could, and the knowledge rubbed salt into the new wound she had created for herself. Instinctively, she had known how ludicrous her accusation had been the moment she'd uttered the damaging words, but it was far too late to try and take them back, and the solid wall now between herself and Jack made it impossible to even offer any kind of an apology.

What made it all so much worse was the way his quiet comment was haunting her. Not the insulting implication that Olivia's appealing attributes had to have come from her father. It was the other comment that had lodged much deeper. He had been misguided enough, he'd said, to fall in love with her. The reminder of Jack's capacity for tenderness that his touch of Stella had evoked sharpened the pain immeasurably.

Jack hadn't been alone. Hannah had also fallen in

love. Head over heels, blindingly happy and quite ready to believe in a future as rosy as a Canterbury sunset could be. Not that any words of love had been spoken aloud. The time frame had been too short but the understanding had been there in every glance. In every excited plan for their new careers and lives. And in every touch.

Especially in every touch. Even now, after more than five years, Hannah could remember exactly what it felt like to be touched by Jack, thanks to reliving that stroke of the cheek as she'd watched him with Stella. Somehow the grief of losing what they'd had so fleetingly had also come back with a vengeance. Maybe it had somehow got mixed up in Stella's tragic case. Knowing that she had to put her personal reactions to one side as she dealt with her work prompted Hannah to turn away from the window. It was unfortunate that her movement coincided with Jack approaching the lifts. Their lines of vision clashed and then held and Hannah had to pull the emotional shutters down with all the strength she had to prevent making a spectacle of herself by bursting into tears. Jack was the one to break the eye contact and he turned away to punch the button and summon the lift without saying a word.

The sad news that Stella had died peacefully in her mother's arms came through on Wednesday morning. Hannah had had two days' practice keeping a firm lid on her own emotions, however, so she knew she wouldn't let the news affect what was shaping up to be a hectic day. Peter Smiley's firm seemed to have a huge list of patients scattered throughout the hospital and as the head of department's morning was being spent in his private practice, Hannah, William and their house surgeons were kept on the run. It was Hannah's responsibility to keep an eye on the overall efficiency of the team.

'Is Angus Bradley still vomiting?'

'Yes.'

'Not projectile, is it?' The eleven-year-old boy had been admitted only an hour ago for observation, having been knocked off his bicycle on his way to school.

'No.'

'There's someone from Neurology due shortly.' Hannah put the case notes on the pile in front of William. 'Do a full neurological check on him every ten to fifteen minutes and watch for any signs of rising intracranial pressure. He's probably going to need a CT.'

Hannah picked up another set of notes. Clare Muir was a ten-year-old girl with juvenile chronic arthritis. 'We're not getting enough response from the non-steroidal anti-inflammatory drugs. I'm going to get a new consult from Rheumatology to consider intra-articular steroids, especially for her knees. We don't want her losing any more mobility if we can help it.' She put Clare's notes on her own pile. 'Sarah can probably be discharged this morning. We've got her asthma well under control again.'

'We're getting a lot of respiratory patients in at the moment, aren't we? Three cases of whooping cough since the weekend.'

Hannah nodded. 'Let's hope it's not the start of a major epidemic.' She eyed the piles of notes on the table. 'I think that's about it for now. Stephen needs his IV replaced again. Can you cope with that?'

William nodded.

'I need to get up to NICU and check that baby with the burns and there's several newborn checks waiting in

Obstetrics. We'll need to try and squeeze them in before the outpatient clinic this afternoon.'

'No rest for the wicked, then.'

Hannah's smile was a trifle grim. 'Let's just hope we don't get any emergency Caesars or repeat admissions on top of everything else.'

Her hope was not fulfilled. Peter had to excuse himself from the clinic while he went to a Caesarean. Hannah visited the emergency department to readmit Harry, a twelve-year-old cystic fibrosis patient whose upper respiratory tract infection was complicating the management of his disease, and William was dispatched to deal with the next call from the emergency department. Hannah looked at her watch when William had gone. She looked at the patients still sitting in the waiting room and sighed as she reached for the phone on her desk and dialled for an outside line.

'Emma? I'm going to be running a bit late tonight. Any chance you could collect Livvy for me and stay with her?'

'Sure. Anything that needs doing at home?'

'You could bring the washing in if it's dry. And feed the hens. If I'm any later than 6.30 you could go ahead with Livvy's bath and story.' Hannah sincerely hoped she wouldn't be any later. Arriving home to find Olivia asleep would completely wipe out her favourite part of the day. Today, in particular, after the news of Stella's death, Hannah needed some time with her own daughter but she couldn't be sorry that the day was so busy. She was too distracted to dwell on the downside of being a paediatrician and the emotional involvement that was inevitable with some of their young patients. She even managed to forget about the problems she had with the new paediatric surgeon.

It was unfortunate that she had to be reminded of both at the point when she had finally finished the outpatient clinic and was ready to admit to her exhaustion and escape home. She had only intended to go to her office for long enough to collect her briefcase, but the angry voices coming from nearby Room 1 couldn't be ignored. Hannah could hear the wail of a frightened child in an adjoining room and saw the horrified stare of a mother who was walking the corridor in an attempt to lull her infant to sleep. She wasn't the only staff member concerned by the unpleasant ruckus. Jack followed her into Room 1 where Hannah found William Price looking at a complete loss to know how to deal with the situation.

Jadine Milton was sitting on the bed in the single room. She was crying miserably and clutching her stomach with both arms, her Barbie doll lying discarded on the end of the bed. A man Hannah didn't recognise was standing beside William and an older woman had raised her voice in response to Jadine's mother's outraged accusations.

'He's her father, Caroline. He has the right to see his own daughter.'

'Like hell he does! If I'd known you were letting that happen, there's no way I would have let Jadie stay with you. How could you *do* that to me, Mum?'

'I've only done what's best for Jadine.'

'She's my kid, too.' The man sounded just as angry as the women. 'You've got no right to stop me seeing her. You were told that by the courts, for God's sake.'

'You gave up your rights when you walked out on us,' Caroline spat. 'Don't think you can swan back in and steal my daughter now because it suits you.'

'It suits you well enough to dump her with your mother when you want to spend time with your—'

'OK, that's enough.' The calm voice carried more than enough authority to silence the group and alert them to the newcomers in the room. 'You can't have this conversation in here,' Jack continued. 'You're disrupting the whole ward.' His tone hardened. 'And I'm sure you can see the effect it's having in here.' He stepped towards the bed. 'Jadine, is that your name?'

'My tummy hurts.' The sobs increased in intensity. Jadine's face was pale but her cheeks were flushed scarlet. Hannah hadn't seen her so upset before and it was hardly surprising.

'Come with me, all of you,' she ordered Jadine's family. 'We can discuss this in my office.'

'I'm not going anywhere with him.' Caroline announced. She folded her arms and glared at Hannah. '*I'm* not leaving *my* daughter.'

'You can stay,' Jack told her curtly. 'I'll stay as well.' His glance at William was supportive. 'Everyone else can go with Dr Campbell, thanks.' He turned back to Jadine and his tone softened. 'It's OK, sweetie. Nobody's cross with you.'

Nobody was going to argue with Jack. Especially Hannah. The relief of seeing Caroline subside quietly into a chair near the window and the other two adults ready to follow her from the room made Jack's interference in her patient's management more welcome than not. At least it was, until Jack caught her leaving her office with her briefcase in her hand nearly an hour later.

'Where are they? The father and grandmother?'

'They've gone home. We've had a good talk.'

'Did you let them know that Jadine probably has appendicitis? That she'll need surgery?'

'Jadine Milton does not need surgery, Jack. This is her fifth admission in the space of two months with recurrent abdominal discomfort. We've tested her for everything under the sun and I think today's episode has confirmed our opinion that her family circumstances are the major contributing factor to these admissions.'

'Really?'

Hannah didn't appreciate the quietly surprised tone. It had been a long and hard day. She had no chance of getting home while Olivia was still awake now, but spending time rehashing the exhaustive investigations her firm had revisited with this patient only a few weeks ago was the last thing she needed.

'Read her notes if you're so interested, Jack, but we haven't requested a surgical consult and we're unlikely to do so. We'll keep Jadine under observation and will then discharge her. As we've done on the previous occasions when her symptoms have resolved with no organic cause being implicated.'

'I've already read her notes,' Jack snapped. 'Including your last entry. You seem to think this is some form of Munchausen's, don't you?'

'The family's dysfunctional,' Hannah shot back. 'The mother has been living her life through her child ever since her husband walked out on the marriage. Until a few months ago, that is, when she started a new relationship. Jadine's ''symptoms'' started shortly after that. Caroline's mother has been filling me in on just what kind of effect that's had on Jadine. It's hardly surprising she needs the security of a bit of extra attention.'

'And that's it? You've made up your mind?' Jack's snort was disbelieving. 'You've got a real bee in your bonnet about any form of child abuse, haven't you, Dr Campbell? Does it *ever* occur to you that you might be misguided?'

It was the perfect opportunity to apologise and there

was no way Hannah could take it. Apologising for her personal remarks would simply be giving Jack licence to question her professional judgement, to dismiss the real efforts she had made to sort out this case. He didn't want a discussion. He wanted another chance to let her know what he thought of her, and Hannah was not about to suffer the accusation of having a closed mind regarding Jadine. Not when she had exhaustively pursued every possibility.

'I've discussed this case with Peter and he agrees that another period of observation is all that's required. William will be monitoring her until 11 p.m.' Hannah turned away. 'I've actually been off duty for two hours now and unless you can come up with a more convincing reason for detaining me, I'm going home.'

Olivia was sound asleep by the time Hannah arrived home at 8 p.m. Disappointment at missing even a cuddle was another black mark for a bad day. The babysitter, Emma Finlay, wasn't to know that she was about to contribute an even larger one.

'Dad's finally decided to sell the farm,' she told Hannah as she gathered her belongings ready to head home. 'It'll go on the market in the next month or two, I expect.'

'Oh, no!' The decision hadn't been unexpected but the timing seemed unfortunate. Hannah's property was only half an acre. She leased another acre from the Finlays and without the extra paddock she would have no room for Joseph.

'Don't worry,' Emma said. 'I'm not going far away. I'll be at university for another couple of years at least and I was planning to go flatting anyway. I'll still need my income from babysitting.'

'That's a relief.' Hannah smiled. 'Now I'll just have to hope the new owners will be happy for me to continue leasing that paddock.'

'Dad said something about that. I'll tell him to ring you when I get home.'

Andrew Finlay rang just as Hannah was half-heartedly picking at her microwaved dinner of chicken and rice.

'I'm on the waiting list for bypass surgery,' he reminded her when she expressed her sadness at having to change neighbours. 'And Jan's sick of worrying about me trying to keep up with the heavy work. You know we rather fancied growing blueberries? Well, we found the perfect property last week and they've accepted our offer.'

'Do you think it'll take long for your place to sell?'

'Long enough to let us sort something out about your paddock,' Andrew said reassuringly. 'I've had a look at the boundaries. If you took an extra five acres or so, it would give you that creek and all the pine trees.'

'I don't need that much land,' Hannah protested. 'And I doubt very much whether I could afford it.'

'It would be difficult to get a boundary change through Council for a smaller area.' Andrew sounded as though he was shaking his head. 'It just wouldn't work, adding the one paddock. Besides, Livvy might want a pony or two in a few years' time and the extra land would add a lot of value to your property.'

'How much would you want?'

Andrew named a figure that made Hannah's heart sink. She had worked so hard to get where she was now. Bumping up her mortgage to that extent would push her well past any comfort zone. Unless…she had the security of a permanent and well paid consultancy position.

'I'll think about it, Andy. I'd love to say yes but I'm

not sure I'll be able to manage. Would a couple of weeks be too long for you to wait for an answer?'

'No problem. You sound tired, Hannah. Make sure you get some rest, won't you?'

Hannah had every intention of following her kindly neighbour's advice but the unexpected phone call at 11.30 p.m. chased any possibility of rest away.

'William! You're supposed to be home by now. What's happened?'

'I tried to ring you a couple of hours ago but your phone was engaged. Jadine Milton's just come out of Theatre.'

'*What?*'

'Perforated appendix,' William reported grimly. 'I called Peter in and we've started IV antibiotics.'

'But... Her presentation was exactly the same as every other admission she's had and appendicitis was the first thing we always looked for. She wasn't running a temperature this time, was she?'

'She spiked one pretty quickly around 9 p.m. That was when I rang you.'

When she had been having her chat with Andrew Finlay. She groaned inwardly. The presentation hadn't been *exactly* the same either. Jadine had been far more upset than usual but what child wouldn't have been, with a family war erupting around her?

'Her pain increased considerably as well,' William continued. 'With guarding and rigidity in the right iliac fossa. I chased up the lab results and her white cell count was way up.'

'None of her previous admissions gave any indication of a grumbling appendix.' Hannah couldn't believe this. 'We did everything short of laparotomy to exclude it.'

'Jack said it was probably coincidence. He went through all her notes pretty thoroughly himself.'

'I'll bet he did.' Hannah was already cringing at the thought of facing Jack tomorrow. 'This is awful, Will. How is Jadine now?'

'The surgery went well. I was invited to go in and watch, which is why I didn't ring again till now. They removed the appendix and cleaned up around it as much as possible. She's been put in ICU overnight to monitor abdominal pressures and she's sedated. She'll be kept nil by mouth for a few days with IV fluids and antibiotic cover. I heard Jack telling the mother that she's going to be fine.'

'Thank God for that,' Hannah murmured. She was still trying to cope with the personal implications of this case. It was a disaster.

William sounded fairly subdued himself. 'Jack said it was a good lesson for me in keeping an open mind. Even if you think it's a case of crying wolf, you've got to take every admission as a fresh start. Especially with kids.'

'Of course.' And that was precisely what Hannah had done with Jadine each time. Until today. By allowing circumstances and prejudice to affect her judgement this time, she could well have endangered a child's life. Jack had been right. She had closed her mind to other possibilities. He had the perfect ammunition to make real trouble for her now.

And she deserved it.

Strangely, nobody seemed to agree with Hannah the next morning.

'It's *not* your fault, Hannah. It was my decision as much as yours to take a wait-and-see approach.' Peter's tone was firm. 'It was reasonable, given her presenting symptoms and her history. These things happen. Acute abdomens are a real problem with children and, given Jadine's previous admissions, this was unfortunate but almost inevitable. Even her family agree with that.'

Even more surprisingly, Jack did not appear interested in taking the opportunity to rub Hannah's nose in the case.

'Her mother was delighted that there was something genuinely wrong this time. She was starting to believe that she was being manipulated by her mother and daughter into giving up her new boyfriend. Having a bit of a crisis brought them all together remarkably well, actually. I think they'll get the whole situation sorted out, thanks to this.'

'I still can't believe I let this happen.' Hannah wasn't ready to accept the comfort. 'I feel dreadful, Jack.'

The raised eyebrow was not entirely without sympathy but his words were cutting. 'It's not the first time, though, is it, Hannah?'

'Look, I've been wanting to apologise for—'

'Save it,' Jack interrupted, holding up his hand. 'It's not going to make any difference. Let's just leave things the way they are, shall we?'

So she was to have no chance to offer an explanation or apology. Was this revenge for the similar way she had once treated him? Fair enough. Hannah swallowed her protest and got on with another busy day.

At least today she managed to get away in plenty of time to collect Olivia herself. The ringing of her mobile phone as she negotiated the rush-hour traffic was a nuisance but not annoying enough to detract from the pleasure of anticipating an evening with her daughter. And she couldn't afford to ignore the call. Hannah had asked to be notified if Jadine's condition gave any cause for

100 THE DOCTOR'S SECRET FAMILY

concern whatsoever. There was no way Hannah was going to be seen to be less than extremely diligent in any further care of this particular patient. She changed down a gear, slowing as she approached a roundabout, and steered with one hand as she answered the call.

'Hannah Campbell.'

'Hannah? Are you still at the hospital?'

'No, I'm on my way to collect Livvy.' Hannah frowned. The voice sounded strained enough to make recognition difficult. 'Is that Lucy?'

'Yes. Livvy's not here, Hannah. That's what I'm ringing to tell you.'

'Where is she?'' Hannah was watching for a gap in the traffic.

'She's with Shirley. They've gone to the hospital. To the emergency department.'

'What?' Hannah had to move forward and she had to change gear with the hand holding the phone. It was a second or two before she could get it close enough to her ear again to hear Lucy. 'Did you say an accident?' she queried tersely. 'Is she all right?'

Stupid question. Shirley wouldn't be on the way to the hospital if Olivia was 'all right'. Hannah was trying to change lanes now in the middle of the roundabout to avoid getting swept off in the wrong direction. She needed to go back the way she'd come. Lucy's reassuring tone was only half registering as Hannah put her indicator on and tried to catch the eye of a male driver who needed to pull back a little to let her in.

'She's fine. And it wasn't even a serious accident anyway. We didn't think anything of it until Ben's caregiver arrived and started panicking.'

'Why?' Hannah had to use both hands to steer as she accelerated to change lanes before she lost the opportunity. She received an irate blast on the horn from the man she'd cut in front of, but ignored it. At least she was travelling back towards the hospital again. She held the phone up to hear that Lucy was still talking rapidly.

'And the arm was getting really swollen and the bruise looked—'

Another car hooted and Hannah realised her indicator was still flashing. She flicked it off. 'I'll have to go, Lucy. I'm on my way back to the hospital. I should be there in ten minutes.'

It was more like fifteen, and Hannah used the first three of them to punch in a rapid-dial number on her phone that put her in direct contact with her head of department.

'Peter? Are you busy?'

'Never too busy for you, Hannah. What's wrong?'

'Livvy's been taken to Emergency. There's been an accident at the day care centre. I'm not sure of the details but could you get down there and keep an eye on what's happening, please? I'm a few minutes away and if she needs to be admitted I would rather it was under you than anybody else.'

'I'm on my way,' Peter said calmly. 'Don't worry, Hannah. I'm sure she'll be fine.'

Hannah wasn't so sure and travelling against the flow of traffic leaving the central city at the end of a working day was slow enough to increase her tension considerably. Why hadn't Shirley rung and informed her of the accident as soon as it had happened? She would still have been at the hospital. She could have advised whether an ambulance needed summoning. Above all, she could have been in the emergency department to meet her probably frightened child.

Olivia had never been to hospital as a patient before.

The thought of her being injured and in pain and surrounded by strangers was too awful to contemplate. Hannah swung her car into a park as close to the emergency department as she could find. She slammed the door closed behind her.

Then she ran towards the building.

CHAPTER SIX

THE emergency department was humming.

Many of the cubicles had their curtains drawn, hiding the occupants, and Hannah had no clue which one might contain her daughter. A registrar appeared from one and Hannah could see a large woman lying on the bed behind him. A nurse flicked another curtain back as she pushed a blood-pressure cuff stand into a cubicle where an elderly man was sitting. Hannah skirted three ambulance stretchers waiting in a line in the triage area. The resuscitation areas used to treat more seriously unwell patients were all in use and all had their curtains drawn. Hannah poked her head into Resus 1 to see an intubation procedure in progress on someone who was clearly in cardiac arrest. A distraught-looking relative was still present and Hannah's own anxiety increased further. Olivia was the only family she had. The only part of her life she couldn't survive without.

She hesitated. Which area should she look into next? It would probably be quicker to try and catch the attention of the busy triage nurse and ask where her daughter was but when Hannah tried, the nurse looked blank.

'Olivia Campbell? I don't think she's here.'

'Four-year-old girl. Blond hair,' Hannah prompted. 'She's been brought in after an accident at a day care centre.'

The nurse shook her head again, her attention rapidly diverted by the patient on the stretcher in front of her as the woman began vomiting. Hannah looked away desperately and saw Peter emerging from Resus 3.

'Peter!' Hannah narrowly missed a collision with a registrar pushing a twelve-lead ECG trolley. 'Where is she? *How* is she?'

'She's fine, Hannah. She hasn't been injured at all.' Peter's hands were on Hannah's shoulders, his grip as reassuring as his tone. 'The woman who runs the centre—Shirley, is it? She said she had to bring Livvy with them because she was so upset at being separated from Ben.'

'Ben?' Hannah was bewildered now. What did Jack's son have to do with this?

'He's Jack Douglas's son. Apparently he goes to the same day care as Livvy. Coincidence, isn't it? Didn't you know how friendly they were with each other?'

'Yes, I knew.' Hannah's nod was impatient. 'But what's *Ben* doing here?'

'He had a bit of a knock. Nothing serious, but with his condition we can't be too careful.'

'What condition?'

'He has Von Willebrand's disease.'

Hannah's brain went into overdrive. Von Willebrand's disease was a bleeding disorder, similar to haemophilia in its reduced factor Vlll activity but differentiated by the mechanism that produced a prolonged bleeding time. Like haemophilia, the degree of severity was highly variable but Hannah had a sudden memory of the bruises on Ben's legs and arm. She could hear his understanding tone when he'd said so matter-of-factly, 'Dad worries about me', and she could just imagine how 'cross' Jack would have been that Ben had been riding Joseph without a helmet.

'He's quite seriously affected, isn't he?' she asked quietly.

Peter nodded. 'He also has the complication of having type IIB Von Willebrand's. He can't be treated with the usual DDAVP regime to increase factor VIII yield so he needs infusions of factor VIII for any more serious bleeds. He's had some now and we're treating the bruise with pressure and ice. We'll admit him overnight, repeat the factor VIII if necessary and get an orthopaedic check tomorrow just to make sure his elbow joint isn't affected.'

Hannah nodded. 'Are his parents with him at the moment?'

Peter gave her a curious glance. 'Ben's mother died years ago. Jack's a solo parent, just like you are. I'm surprised you didn't know that. He talks about Ben all the time to anyone that wants to listen.'

'I guess I don't talk to him that much,' Hannah said evasively. 'Not about his personal life, anyway.' She had, in fact, deliberately avoided even a casual conversation with anybody who might have given her information about Jack's wife. She hadn't wanted to know. She had just assumed she was beautiful and well groomed and needed a nanny to help care for their son probably because she was too busy spending time keeping herself beautiful and well groomed.

Hannah felt ashamed of the shallow and critical assumption she had harboured. She also felt ashamed of keeping such a stony distance between herself and Jack as she'd tried to keep her own personal life private. She could easily have found out about his solo parent status. She could just as easily have found out the cause of Ben's physical condition. She hadn't bothered asking. She hadn't been prepared to listen.

'Jack's with him, of course,' Peter was saying now. 'And Livvy's in there as well, but we sent Shirley away. She took the nanny home. Poor girl was upset. She seemed to think it was her fault that the school hadn't sent Ben's medical records through to the centre. She'd assumed they knew about Ben's condition which was why she hadn't said anything. Still, it's all sorted now and Jack took responsibility for the communication breakdown. It won't happen again.'

'He should be wearing a Medic Alert bracelet.' If he had, Hannah would have noticed it. She would have understood why Ben looked like a battered child and the finger marks on Ben's arm which had seemed so damning could well have been attributed to the result of a playground game or maybe an adult catching hold of him to prevent a more serious injury. Above all, she would never have made the dreadful suggestion to his father that Ben was being physically abused. She could very easily imagine the effect that would have had on a parent who already had to contend with a potentially serious condition suffered by his child. No wonder he'd been too disgusted to bother enlightening her. Hannah wasn't sure she wanted to go anywhere near Jack right now but Peter was tilting his head invitingly.

'Come and see them.'

'I should just take Livvy home. Can you bring her out for me?'

Peter shook his head with a smile. 'I wouldn't want to try. Anyway, you've got to see this. It's pretty cute.'

Hannah could understand his smile when she stepped through the curtains into Resus 3. Ben was sitting on the bed, a cold pack and pressure bandage swathing his upper right arm. Jack was sitting on the chair beside the bed, busy filling in some paperwork. Right alongside

Ben, cross-legged on the bed, was a small girl, holding tightly onto the fingers of Ben's left hand, well away from the IV cannula bandaged in place on top of his hand. It was Olivia who spotted Hannah's arrival first.

'Hello, Mummy! Ben got *hurt*.' Her intonation suggested a wealth of suffering.

'I know, darling. How are you, Ben?'

'I'm OK,' Ben said calmly. 'My arm's a bit sore.'

'He was pushing me on the swing,' Olivia told Hannah. 'And Blake wanted a turn and Ben said he had to wait.' Her tone became outraged. 'And Blake got cross and pushed Ben and we had a *crash*.'

'Oh, dear!' Hannah was deliberately avoiding the stare she could feel coming from Jack.

'We've got a bed ready for you upstairs, Ben,' Peter said. 'There's even a bed for Dad if he wants to stay with you tonight.'

'*I* want to stay with Ben tonight,' Olivia announced firmly.

Peter raised an eyebrow at Hannah and his lips twitched. 'Ben is Olivia's friend,' he said gravely. 'She loves him very much.'

Hannah had to look at Jack finally. His expression held the same sort of resignation she was feeling. They might not like what was happening between their children but the pull was obviously too powerful to break. There was something else to be read in those dark eyes as well. Maybe the punishment that Hannah was suffering, having learned of Ben's condition, was a little harsh even in the face of how misguided and hurtful her accusations had been.

'Maybe Livvy could stay and visit for a while,' she suggested hesitantly. 'I'd be happy to go and collect whatever Ben needs from home if you want to stay with him, Jack.'

'I have a better idea,' Jack responded. 'Why don't you *and* Livvy stay with Ben. I'll get his P.Js and games console and things from home. I could pick up some hamburgers or something equally gross for dinner on my way back.'

'Cool!' Ben clearly approved of the plan. 'Can I have some chips and a milkshake, too?'

'Sure.'

'Can *I* have some chips?' Olivia's face shone with hope as she turned it towards Jack. 'Pleeeease?'

'Sure.' Jack's smile seemed a little reluctant as though he had tried but had been unable to prevent it surfacing. His glance at Hannah was questioning.

'Livvy doesn't get chips very often,' she explained. 'It's a special treat.'

Jack's smile broadened as he found Olivia's eyes still fastened on him. 'Would you like a hamburger, too, Livvy?'

The look of sheer glee that Ben and Olivia exchanged made all the adults smile, and Peter chuckled.

'I'll leave you to it. Call me if you're worried, otherwise I'll see Ben first thing in the morning.'

'I'll head off, too.' Jack rose and ruffled Ben's curls as he left. 'Back soon, buddy.'

He paused as he passed Hannah. 'I've got my mobile with me,' he said, 'but I'm sure you'll take good care of our kids.'

'Of course.' Hannah watched him disappear through the gap in the curtains.

Our kids.

If only he knew.

The thought that followed instantaneously was even more powerful.

He *had* to know.

He should have known right from the start. Giving up any effort to inform him had not been the only injustice Hannah had dealt Jack, but at least it was one she could put right. She had no right to punish Jack by excluding him from Olivia's life. He had the right to know the truth, just as Olivia had the right to know who her father was and that she and Ben were half-siblings. It could be why these children had found such a bond with each other and it was a connection they deserved to maintain.

It wasn't a question of whether she should tell Jack any more.

It was simply a question of *when*.

Sharing the take-away meal in the privacy of Ben's room on the ward was definitely not the right time. The impulse faded somewhat as Hannah watched and listened to Jack interact with his son. Their bond was obviously a very close one. As close as the one she shared with Olivia. How long had he been a solo parent? What had happened to Ben's mother and why had Jack denied having a son in the first place? Hannah could do the arithmetic. Ben had been at least two years old when she had met Jack.

Questions piled onto each other and Hannah's curiosity increased. So did a feeling of apprehension. What difference could the knowledge of Olivia's paternity have on the bond between Jack and Ben? She needed to find some answers to at least some of her questions before dropping a bombshell like this on Jack. Her gaze became more focused as she tried to gauge what his reaction might be. He was clearly used to coping as a solo parent and the love he had for his son was equally transparent.

Was being a solo father harder than being a solo mother? Men were expected to have careers. A full-time job and using child care would be accepted as a necessity, rather than the luxury some people viewed it to be in her case. But Jack had had more to contend with than most solo parents with regard to his child's health. A hospital admission did not seem to have fazed either of them. Ben still had a pressure bandage on his arm and a sling to rest the limb. His other hand was bandaged to protect the IV port through which he would receive further medication, but he was digging into his hamburger and fries as though nothing was amiss. He had sized up the ward when Hannah had given him a guided tour on his arrival and it had clearly passed muster.

'There's cool toys in the play room,' he informed Jack. 'And there's videos. They've got *The Lion King* on at the moment.'

'I *love* Simba,' Olivia announced.

Jack smiled. 'You love lots of things, don't you, Livvy?'

Olivia's happy grin was framed by tomato sauce, some of which had travelled to her wispy blond curls. 'I love Ben,' she confirmed. 'And I love Joe and Sooty and Snow.' She took a deep breath. 'And I love Shirley and Lucy and Suzanne and Horace...even though he's grumpy sometimes.'

'Who's Horace?' Jack's eyebrows had been rising steadily as he'd listened to the growing list.

'The goat,' Hannah supplied.

'And I love Arthur and Bianca and Carla and Deirdre and Elsa.' Olivia chanted on, the remains of her hamburger forgotten. She paused thoughtfully for a moment.

'And I love Mummy,' she added with finality. She turned wide brown eyes towards the child sitting beside her on the bed. 'Who do *you* love, Ben?'

'Just Dad,' he said offhandedly. 'And you, I guess.'

Olivia beamed. Then she looked at the rest of her hamburger. 'I can't eat any more, Mummy. I'm *f'lup*.'

'We'd better go and wash the sauce off your face, then, darling. Let's go to the bathroom.'

'I know where it is.' Ben was climbing off the bed. 'I'll take her.'

'What about the rest of your milkshake?' Jack caught the container as it tipped dangerously on the side of the bed.

'I'm full up, too,' Ben said. 'And I want to see if *The Lion King* is finished yet.'

'OK, but don't be long,' Jack instructed. 'I want to take that bandage off your arm soon and see what that bruise is doing.'

'It doesn't hurt any more.' Ben was waiting for Olivia to scramble off the bed. 'It'll just look bad.'

Jack stood up to help Olivia slide to the floor. She wriggled free of his hands with her attention still firmly focused on Ben. 'I got a big bruise on *my* arm when Horace bit me,' she told him. 'It was *black*.'

Hannah watched her daughter trail in Ben's wake as they left the room, but the realisation that she was alone with his father took time to sink in. She was thinking about bruises. About Von Willebrand's disease. Haemophilia was carried by females and almost always manifested itself in males. Von Willebrand's disease was an autosomal dominant trait that could be carried by males and inherited by both males and females. Had it come from Jack? Did the fact that Olivia bruised easily have nothing to do with her fair skin? The idea that

Olivia could have a medical condition Hannah had been unaware of was disturbing, but she couldn't afford to consider the implications right now.

And there was no need for alarm. Even if Olivia had inherited a tendency for prolonged bleeding, it was mild enough to have been unnoticeable and it was therefore highly unlikely to be significant. It was simply something to be aware of for the future. Definitely not right now. Not when any hint of concern could alert Jack to something she was not quite ready to tell him. Hannah turned her gaze away from the disappearing children, determinedly marshalling her thoughts. She found Jack watching her again.

'They've really hit it off, haven't they?'

Hannah nodded. 'I'm afraid Livvy gets fairly passionate about what and who she chooses to love.'

'I've noticed.' Jack's smile was crooked. 'You're not bothered that you were last on the list, then?'

Hannah smiled back. 'Not a bit. It's easy to take the things closest to you for granted. Especially when you're only four.'

'Ben's list was a bit limited, wasn't it?' Jack sounded thoughtful. 'I'll have to do something about getting him a pet. It's always been on the list for when we got really settled, but he's been talking about your animals nonstop since that visit.'

The reminder couldn't be ignored. 'I'm sorry about what I said that night, Jack. I had no idea of Ben's condition.'

'Of course you didn't.'

'It was a reasonable concern but it hadn't come from me initially. It was Shirley who noticed those bruises.'

Jack nodded. 'She told me. She also told me that you advised her not to leap to any conclusions. She should be commended for her concern, in fact. It was my fault that the relevant information wasn't passed on.'

'If Ben wore a Medic Alert bracelet it would help.'

Jack nodded again. 'It's been ordered. It's one of the many things on the "get sorted" list. There's been rather a lot of them, what with shifting countries.'

'Anyway, I *am* sorry.'

Jack looked away as he shrugged. 'You're not the first person to make that particular assumption. I would have been surprised if you hadn't.'

Hannah was silent for a moment. At least she had finally managed to make an apology, even if its acceptance had been less than gracious. The personal criticism of having a closed mind was easy to infer but she let it pass. She *had* made assumptions about Jack's wife, hadn't she? It was tempting to escape the discomfort of the atmosphere by using the children as an excuse to leave the room, but Hannah could recognise the opportunity she now had to satisfy just a little of her escalating curiosity.

'I had no idea you were a solo parent. That first day we met on the ward I asked if you had brought your family with you this time and you said yes.'

'Ben is my family.'

'But a "family" normally implies more than one parent.'

'Only if you're inclined to make assumptions.'

Hannah was reduced to silence again but she couldn't let the dig pass for the second time. 'Any assumptions I make are generally based on experience. I'm not blindly prejudiced, Jack.'

'You are if you refuse to open your eyes.'

'What's that supposed to mean?'

Jack leaned back in his chair. 'Well, take our conversation the day I arrived. You mentioned the day care centre you used for Olivia, and when I asked about it you assumed I was criticising you for having a career and leaving other people to care for your child.'

'You sounded critical.' Hannah eyed Jack suspiciously. Of course she had assumed criticism. She had fielded that kind of response from far too many people over the years. The evidence that Jack had interpreted her response so accurately was a little unnerving.

'No. If anything, I probably sounded surprised. I was actually delighted. I don't leap in to criticise anybody and I know better than most that child care can be a necessity rather than choice. I couldn't support my child if I didn't work.' Jack's sigh sounded weary. 'If I'd thought this through more carefully I would have taken longer to try and get settled before I started work. The day I met you I was still hunting desperately for the kind of child care assistance I needed, and a personal recommendation was just what I was after. If you hadn't made that assumption, you could have avoided feeling criticised. You could also have been helpful, which might have got us started again on a much better footing.'

Hannah swallowed. There was no way they were going to start again. She wouldn't want to. Would she?

'You ended up using the same place, anyway.'

'Bit of a coincidence, wasn't it?'

'Why did you pick Maysfield?'

'Ben and I spent a day looking at a few schools. Maysfield was on the edge of town and the school's playing field borders paddocks with cows in them. Ben's grown up in a large city and the look on his face when he saw the cows watching the kids playing football made the decision easy. We found a flat to rent and it was the school that let me know about the after-school service Shirley was starting.' His glance at Hannah suggested that her curiosity might be contagious. 'What made you live so far out of town? Did you marry a rural GP?'

Hannah laughed. 'Now who's making assumptions?'

'It was a guess, not an assumption,' Jack retorted.

'No, it was definitely an assumption. What's more, it's exactly the same assumption I made about you with less of a reason to make it than I had.'

'You mean…*you're* a solo parent?'

Hannah was impressed again at Jack's ability to interpret her response. 'I'm surprised you didn't know. It's not something I've ever tried to hide. Everyone around here knows.'

'I've avoided talking about you,' Jack admitted. 'You were already giving me a hard time and I didn't want anyone finding out the reason why. I think they assumed you just didn't like the look of me and it seemed safer to leave it like that.'

'Sometimes assumptions *are* safer.'

'And I guess we do all make them to some extent, consciously or not.' Jack eyed Hannah intently. 'So it didn't work out, then? With Olivia's father?'

'That pretty much sums things up.'

'That's a shame.'

Hannah met his gaze. 'Things don't always work out the way we might want them to.'

'No.' Jack held the eye contact and they both knew what they were really talking about here. 'They don't, do they? Sometimes we just have to pick up the pieces and make the best of what we've got.'

Hannah nodded slowly. 'Peter told me your wife died a few years ago. Ben's a credit to you, Jack. He's a neat kid.'

Jack smiled. 'He's great, isn't he?' His smile faded rapidly. 'And Ben's mother was someone else's wife when she died. *Not* mine.'

The reminder of the first assumption Hannah had ever made about Jack hung in the air between them heavily enough to smother any further conversation. The increasingly awkward silence was broken by the return of the children to the room and then there was no way to continue the exchange that had provoked more questions than it had provided answers. And Hannah wanted more answers. It was past time to get Olivia home to bed but Hannah didn't want to go without leaving some kind of invitation to continue the contact they had established.

'It would be great if Ben could come and visit again one day.' Hannah caught Jack's gaze. 'I can assure you I won't let him ride without a helmet.'

Olivia was insisting on giving Ben a farewell kiss, which was clearly suffered with some embarrassment. Ben scrubbed his cheek with his bandaged hand but then caught Jack's wink and grinned.

'I'd really like to ride Joe again, Dad. And Livvy and I want to build that hut in the hedge.'

'We'll sort something out,' Jack said casually. 'Now, let's have a look at that arm, buddy.'

That some kind of truce had been tacitly agreed upon between Hannah and Jack became quickly apparent to even casual observers.

'If you call in a surgical consult on every abdo pain we see,' William observed, 'people are going to start talking about you and Jack.'

'I just don't want to see a repeat of Jadine Milton's case,' Hannah defended herself.

'And Jack doesn't seem to mind.' William grinned. 'So you'll get him in to see Larissa, then?'

Hannah glanced at the clock. 'We'll see how she goes over the next hour or so. The abdo pain seems vague at the moment and could well be due to the upper respiratory tract infection, but just because she's got a dose of bronchiolitis doesn't rule out the possibility of concomitant appendicitis. The incidence of perforation is higher in young children, too. A two-year-old can go from apparent normality to perforation in as little as six hours.'

She slotted the notes back into the trolley and led the way to the next patient on her list. 'Jack will be on with ward when he gets out of Theatre soon, anyway. He wants to see Jadine again before we discharge her and I'll have a chat to him about Larissa at the same time.'

Peter was more forthright. 'You've stopped biting Jack's head off lately,' he observed. 'You even complimented him on his management of that colectomy case. I know I'm notoriously slow to catch up on what happens in people's personal lives around here, but is there something I should know about?'

'Not at all.' Peter was the only staff member who had been aware that Jack and Hannah had met previously, and he had mercifully forgotten about it with the same ease with which he forgot things like the ages of his colleagues' children. 'He's an excellent surgeon,' Hannah added blandly. 'It's hard not to be impressed with his work. You know how hard it's been to manage Theo's ulcerative colitis. He's been a frequent flyer around here for years now. Jack's surgery may well have cured him.'

'Hmm.' Peter wasn't convinced. 'So there's no personal reason why you're looking so smart today, then?'

'Oh, for goodness' sake! This suit is *years* old, Peter.' Nearly six years to be precise. Had Jack recognised the tailored navy jacket and skirt? 'I've got my first interview with the appointing committee this afternoon.'

'Ah.' Peter nodded. 'Of course. Don't worry, Hannah. I'm sure they're going to be just as impressed with your track record as you seem to be with Jack's.'

Shirley saw the exchange between Jack and Hannah at 7 a.m. one morning as they dropped their children at the day care centre.

'You two seem to be getting on very well,' she observed. 'It wouldn't be the first time a couple of kids have brought their single parents together.'

'Jack was just congratulating me,' Hannah told her matter-of-factly. 'I got the consultancy job at the hospital.'

'Oh, that's fantastic! You must be thrilled.'

'I am.' Hannah did not need to pretend indifference now. 'It's just the kind of security Livvy and I needed. I can go ahead and buy that paddock for Joseph now and I'll have more time with Livvy as well. I'm going to work my seven-tenths by doing four days a week, and my head of department is very supportive about helping with any on-call hassles.'

'Just as well. I think Ben's dad is having a bit of bother now that his nanny's resigned.' Shirley sighed. 'I can't help feeling partly responsible for that. She decided she couldn't handle the responsibility after Ben had to go to hospital last week. Jack's keen to try and manage by himself as much as he can. We can help out if he gets caught on weekdays but there's not much we can do about weekends.'

'I've offered to help.' Hannah was careful to sound casual again. 'Jack and I do work together after all and Ben and Livvy are such good friends. Ben will be able to come and play at our house if Jack needs a babysitter on my days off.'

'He's coming this Saturday, isn't he?' Shirley smiled at Hannah's expression. 'You'd be surprised what we hear about at news time. She's very excited.'

Hannah grinned. 'She's ordered a sunny day so they can be outside. They're planning to build a hut.'

The hut was virtually complete by the time Jack arrived at four on Saturday afternoon to take Ben home.

'Oh, no!' Hannah watched him approach from her seat on the verandah steps. 'You're not supposed to be here yet.'

Jack loosened his tie. 'Do you make all your visitors feel this welcome?'

Hannah laughed. 'Sorry. But the kids are having such fun and I've just promised them a picnic tea in the new hut. Are you in a hurry?'

'Not really.' Jack sat down on the edge of the steps. He pulled his tie free and unbuttoned the top of his shirt. 'Hot, isn't it?'

'I'm cooking,' Hannah admitted. 'But I've been working hard. I got commandeered to saw off all the dead branches inside the macrocarpa hedge so there was room for the furniture.'

'Furniture?''

'A little table and chairs from Livvy's old playhouse. I think they've taken a mat and some cushions from the sunroom but I said no to the mattress from the daybed.'

She rubbed at her arms. 'I'm shredded,' she said ruefully. 'Dead macrocarpa's very scratchy.' Hannah
flicked Jack a quick glance. 'Ben's fine. He did help with
some of the sawing and hammering but I kept a close
eye on things.'

'I wasn't about to criticise,' Jack said mildly. 'I don't
wrap Ben up in cotton wool. It's fantastic that Ben's got
the chance to get into normal little-boy activities. It was
one of the main reasons for us coming to live in New
Zealand. I wanted him to have the kind of freedom and
space I used to dream of when I was a kid.'

'Where did you grow up?'

'In Birmingham. Same as Ben.'

Hannah was trying to dust some of the grime from
her bare knees. She had planned to clean herself up a
bit and change out of her old shorts and T-shirt before
Jack returned to collect Ben, but he hadn't seemed to
notice her appearance. He was too busy gazing around
the garden, taking in the huge old walnut tree and the
view into the orchard beyond where Joseph's head could
be seen hanging over a gate as he waited patiently for
the children to take some notice of him. Several of the
hens could be seen beneath one of the old fruit trees
now sporting a cloud of pink blossom and the peaceful
silence was broken by the not-too-distant sound of child-
ish voices and a peal of Olivia's contagious laughter.
Jack smiled.

'This is an amazing spot you've found, Hannah. A
little bit of heaven.'

'We love it.' The we had to include Ben now as well.
His excitement in planning and directing the hut-
building project had been delightful and his pride on
completion would be something Jack would enjoy sharing. Hannah scrambled to her feet.

'Come and see the hut,' she invited. 'They might be ready to welcome visitors by now.'

The children were more than ready to show off the hut but they were nowhere near ready to be separated.

'But we haven't had tea,' Ben said in dismay.

'You *promised*, Mummy. You were going to cook a sausage on the barbecue and we could have 'mato *sauce* and everything.'

'I did promise,' Hannah admitted. She smiled at Jack. 'Could I interest you in a barbecue dinner? I've got a beer or two tucked away in the fridge.'

Jack hesitated for only a moment. 'Tell you what,' he decided. 'I'll go home and change into something cooler. I could pick up a bottle of wine on the way back and maybe a steak or two. That way the kids can have as long as they like to keep playing.'

Any reluctance on Hannah's part to embrace the suggestion was well hidden by the enthusiastic response from both children. She should be looking forward to an opportunity to talk to Jack, she reminded herself during her two-minute shower and a change into clean clothes. The truce that had appeared and grown since Ben's night in hospital ten days ago had given her just the base she needed to find answers to all those lurking questions. Especially one. The 'why Jack had denied having a child' one. But Hannah found herself becoming increasingly nervous as she waited for Jack's return. She could no doubt find the opportunity to ask that particular question this evening, but she wasn't so sure she wanted the answer now.

The truce had done more than give Hannah a good working relationship with Jack. It had allowed her to let go of the last vestiges of resentment and anger his surprise appearance had stirred. It had allowed her to accept as much blame as she'd always given him. It had also allowed the return of a suggestion she had never been entirely able to reject. That Jack hadn't told her he'd had a child because, for some reason, he hadn't known himself. If she asked that question and that suspicion was confirmed then Hannah had some not very pleasant truths about herself she would have to face. Part of her knew that reckoning was unavoidable.

She just wasn't sure she was ready to face it tonight.

CHAPTER SEVEN

THERE was more than one truth waiting to confront Hannah.

The first was unexpected. Overwhelming. It happened in an instant and it changed everything.

Hannah was reaching for the wineglass Jack had just filled for her. Ben and Olivia were heading into the dim interior of the hut to demolish their plates of bread and butter, sausages and sauce.

'Look!' They both heard Olivia's delighted squeal. 'We've got *green* fizzy drink!'

Then came the mature and thoughtful response from Ben. 'Cool. Don't spill it on your bread, Livvy. It'll go soggy and yucky.'

Hannah's hand had reached the wineglass at this point and her gaze had reached Jack's. They were both smiling as they listened to the children.

And then time seemed to stop.

Hannah's hand was on the glass but Jack didn't release it. And neither of them could release the eye contact. Hannah could see the twinkle of amusement in the dark depths of Jack's eyes and she could see what lay beneath. The struggle to manage as a solo parent and the worry about health issues. The kinds of things all parents faced but heightened by having to cope alone. And she could see that none of that mattered because the love he had for his son made it all more than worthwhile. Hannah understood perfectly and the connection was profound.

Profound enough for Hannah to realise, beyond any shadow of doubt, that her love for Jack had never died. It had been buried, shovelled beneath distrust and anger and resentment, but it was still there and that moment of connection had unearthed a glimpse of that shining treasure. Its brilliance was blinding and Hannah was more shaken than she would allow herself to admit. She wrenched her gaze away from Jack's eyes and her hand away from the contact of his fingers. More than a little wine slopped over the edge of the glass.

'Oops, that was a bit of waste,' she said lightly. 'It's not often I get to drink such a good red wine either.'

Hannah could tell Jack was still watching her in the tiny silence that followed. She moved to sit on the low brick wall bordering the courtyard and Jack turned back to the barbecue.

'How do you like your steak?'

'On the well-done side of medium,' Hannah said decisively. 'I hate it looking like it's going to leap off the plate when I poke it with my fork.'

Jack laughed and the moment of tension vanished. He probably hadn't noticed anything, Hannah decided. There was no way to turn the clock back, and if she was capable of feeling the same way about Jack as she had when she had first met him then it was her problem and she needed to deal with it. There was no way Jack would still harbour the same feelings for her. Not if what she suspected about Ben was true. Hannah took a long swallow of the smooth red wine as she watched Jack turn the sizzling steaks over. Maybe now *was* the time to find out. Nothing else she could learn this evening would rock her any more than what she had just discovered.

'Ben's arm seems to be fine,' she ventured. 'That bruise has almost faded completely.'

Jack nodded. He put down the tongs and reached for his own wineglass. 'His coagulation profile is improving slowly with age. He might end up being almost normal. Like me.'

'*You* have Von Willebrand's?'

'It's never been a major issue. I have a more common variety than Ben. I have to be a bit careful when it comes to dental work or minor surgery, but I can just use a DDAVP nasal spray. Fortunately, I've never had a bad accident of any kind.'

'But Ben has?'

'That's how he was diagnosed. He fell down a couple of concrete steps when he was about two. He was taken to hospital by ambulance and luckily got assessed by a team that was clued up enough to realise they had something a little unusual to deal with.'

Hannah summoned her courage. 'And that was why they needed to contact you…when you were away in Auckland?'

'No. That was something rather more serious.' Jack turned the gas flame on the barbecue down to a mere glimmer. 'These are almost ready. Are you hungry?'

Hannah barely registered the query. 'So what was it about, then? The phone call. Your mother-in-law said your son needed you.'

Jack's glance was challenging. 'Are you sure you want to know?'

Hannah swallowed hard. There was a contented silence emanating from the direction of the hut that indicated the children were still busy eating. They had at least a few moments' privacy and…yes, it was high time Hannah knew. She nodded slowly.

Jack stepped away from the barbecue. He came and sat down on the wall beside Hannah, leaving enough of a gap to avoid physical contact. For a moment he seemed to be considering the wine he swirled slowly in his glass.

'Cheryl hadn't been my mother-in-law for years when she made that call. I suspect she used the title to make sure she got put through to me.' Jack swallowed a mouthful of the wine and Hannah had to wait several more heartbeats before he spoke again.

'I met Donna in my final year of med school when I was doing a run in the emergency department. She was a student nurse. She was only twenty when we got married and far too young to know what she really wanted. We separated three years later. She'd been having an affair with a cop by the name of Mike Sullivan for months by then.'

Sullivan. Hannah nodded as she realised its significance. The name on Ben's birth certificate.

'The day the divorce papers came through, Donna turned up on my doorstep. She was upset. Said she didn't want the divorce after all. She wanted *me*.' Jack snorted derisively. 'What she didn't say until the next morning was that she just wanted to make sure she wasn't going to miss anything about me. She went back to Mike and I heard they got married a few weeks later. Then they had a baby. I actually met Donna pushing the pram through a local supermarket one day and she told me Ben was three months old. He was actually five months old.' Jack's tone became harsh. 'Donna had known all along that he could have been mine. She lied about his age and let me assume he was Mike's son.' He paused for only a moment. 'I'll *never* forgive her for that.'

Hannah drained the rest of her wine in a single gulp. He would never forgive her in that case because what she had done was far worse. She knew quite unequivocally that Olivia was his child. And she had as good as lied about his daughter's age with the express intention of misleading him. The wine couldn't begin to wash away the sick feeling settling in her stomach.

'I might never have known the truth if it hadn't been for that accident on the concrete steps. The blood screen they ran showed up the Von Willebrand's disease and subsequent follow-up included a check on other family members, including Ben's parents. Mike Sullivan discovered that he wasn't Ben's father after all.

'He wasn't happy,' Jack continued wryly. 'The fight they had terminated when he pushed Donna down a rather longer set of steps than Ben had fallen down.' He drained his own glass of wine. 'They kept her on life support for a week or so. Long enough for Donna's mother to decide she wasn't going to ruin her life by trying to raise a grandson she didn't want. She knew about the night Donna had spent with me and put two and two together quickly enough. She rang that night to let me know that the life support was being switched off, and that if I wanted to keep my son from going into foster-care I'd better get home and sign a few papers.'

'Oh…' Hannah's quiet sound was a groan. Her chin was almost on her chest and her empty wineglass dangled from a limp hand. 'And there was my note, telling you that you were a bastard. That I never wanted to see or speak to you again. Telling you to go home to your wife and child.'

'It was understandable,' Jack said unexpectedly. 'I was devastated at the time but I had too much else to deal with right then. When I finally had time to think it through, I realised that it was my own fault. You'd asked me straight out if I had a wife or kids lurking anywhere, and I'd said no.'

Hannah nodded silently. They had been lying under

the stars on One Tree Hill. Jack had kissed her and Hannah had known how close she'd been to falling irrevocably in love. All she'd needed had been the reassurance that there had been no demons waiting to confront her and spoil this…as they had done before. Jack's response to her query had echoed louder than anything else over the years.

'I knew I was in love with you,' Jack said softly. 'Using that moment to talk about an ex-wife seemed almost sacrilege. I couldn't do it and I didn't think it mattered. I thought we had the rest of our lives to share any lessons from past mistakes.'

Hannah looked up, knowing that her own pain was in every line of her face. The mistakes Jack had made were nothing compared to hers.

'I tried to tell you. I wrote to you. Twice. I thought you'd just sent the letters back unopened.'

'I thought you'd done that as well,' Hannah said sadly. 'I wrote to you, too. I sent it to the paediatric surgical department at National Children's Hospital.'

'What did your letter say?' Jack's expression was guarded. Maybe he expected the letter to have been an extension of the damning note she'd left in the motel room.

Hannah opened her mouth to answer Jack. To tell him the truth, even knowing that she would be repeating the same betrayal Donna had dealt him. She could do nothing less because he had suffered far more than she had, and the truth was all she could offer now. But she never had the chance to speak. Unnoticed, the children had left their hut.

'We're f'lup, Mummy.'

'What's that horrible smell?' Ben asked.

Jack groaned. 'Our steaks aren't on the well done side of medium, I'm afraid, Hannah. They're cremated.'

'Never mind. I'm not actually very hungry anymore.'

Olivia set the plate she was carefully holding on the ground. She picked up the half-eaten sausage it contained and held it out to Jack.

'It's only got a little bit of green fizzy drink on it,' she said invitingly. 'You can have it, 'cos I'm f'lup.'

'Thanks, Livvy.' Jack's voice sounded oddly gruff. The smile he directed at Hannah was curiously wobbly. 'She's special, isn't she?'

Hannah blinked back tears. The bond between father and daughter was already there. How much stronger would it become if they knew the truth? She had to bite her lip to stop herself saying anything. Ben was here as well. He'd been Jack's only child for five years. How would he feel if he had to share his father with Olivia? Hannah watched Jack respond to the cuddle Olivia offered after the half-eaten sausage had been accepted. Ben was smiling and Hannah had to turn away.

They could have been a family.

It was her fault that they weren't.

Jack's face was being tickled by wispy blond curls but he'd seen the look on Hannah's face as she'd turned away and something inside him melted. She knew the truth now finally, and he had taken responsibility for what had happened between them. She didn't hate him anymore. In fact, Jack had the strong impression that she still had feelings for him. Strong feelings. Maybe, if he wanted to, he could start again with Hannah.

There was something still left of what they had discovered they had all those years ago. And there was something new—their children and the bond already forged between them. He had brought Ben to New Zealand to start a new life. Could Hannah and Olivia be part of that? Did he want them to be?

Oh, yes. There was no doubt about that. Jack had known the moment he'd met Hannah that she would be the only woman he could ever feel so strongly about. He had another chance here and if his instincts were to be trusted, Hannah wanted him to take it.

'I've got a day off tomorrow,' he said. 'Ben and I are going to drive to Akaroa and go on a boat to see the dolphins. Would you like to come with us, Livvy?'

'Oh…*yes-s-s*!' Small arms wound themselves more firmly around Jack's neck.

'Would Mummy like to come, too?' Jack was looking at Hannah over the top of the blond curls but it was Olivia who answered.

'*Yes*,' she said.

Jack's expression apologised for not checking with Hannah first but she was laughing. 'I'd love to come, thanks, Jack. It sounds like fun.'

It *was* fun. The drive to Akaroa with Ben and Olivia singing songs in the back seat and playing 'I Spy'. The walk around the quaint French settlement to admire the lighthouse and craft shops. The boat ride to the mouth of the harbour with the excitement of the frolicking pod of Hector's dolphins that presented themselves. And most of all, the sunshine of the late spring afternoon when Jack and Hannah lay sprawled on towels on the small, sandy beach while Ben and Olivia splashed in the gentle waves.

It was a magic day. A family day. And what made it perfect was the moment Jack took hold of Hannah's hand and then turned towards her. The bright warmth of the sunshine was completely different to that starry night so long ago but the kiss was exactly the same. At least, it would have been had it been allowed to continue for more than the briefest touch. The constraints of their public situation and the potential audience of their children couldn't be forgotten.

The promise was there, however. And the desire. And the understanding that it was only a matter of time until they could find a way to be together alone, if that was what they both wanted. It was probably just as well that finding that time proved frustratingly difficult. It gave them both time to be sure and it gave Hannah the opportunity to reconcile the fact that she hadn't yet told Jack about Olivia. He had waited five years to find out after all. A little more time couldn't hurt. And there were other things Jack should know about Hannah as well. He needed to know why she had acted the way she had. He needed to know about Paul.

'I met him when I was twenty-five,' she told him one evening over dinner. Ben coming home with Hannah and Olivia when Jack was held up in the evenings had become a pleasant habit in the space of only a couple of weeks. Jack staying for dinner when he came to collect Ben looked set to become another enjoyable part of their routine.

'He was a cardiologist here. I fell in love and we moved in together. We couldn't get married until his divorce came through but that didn't bother me. He'd said it was over. Had been for years.'

'But it wasn't?' Jack stopped eating. He was listening carefully and his expression revealed his usual astuteness in interpreting an unspoken message.

Hannah's gaze wandered for a moment but they were still alone. Ben and Olivia had gone out to the hut with a torch. It had a shelf out there now, which Ben had nailed between stout branches. Most of Olivia's old picture books had migrated outside and what Ben couldn't read Olivia was happy to recite from memory.

'I knew he still saw her occasionally. There were legal things that needed deciding and hassles with the house that he spent time sorting out. I didn't know that he'd started sleeping with her again until months later when he told me he was going back to her.'

Jack nodded slowly. 'And you decided you would never have anything to do with another man who had a wife or even an ex-wife tucked away.'

'Actually, I decided I'd had it with men, full stop.' Hannah's smile was grim. 'I watched my father bounce off with other women more than once as I grew up. I lived with the unhappiness he caused every time he left and I could never understand why my mother would let him come back. She said she still loved him, no matter what. And I was so miserable when Paul left, I could finally understand. I knew I wasn't going to make the same mistake my mother had, though, and I got over Paul completely,' Hannah said decisively. 'I spent well over a year believing there was no way I'd ever let myself fall in love again.'

'And then?' Jack's smile was poignant. He already knew the answer.

'And then I met you.'

'And then you found I wasn't as unattached as I'd claimed to be.' Jack was silent for a long moment. 'You must have been very angry.'

'I was devastated,' Hannah admitted. 'I couldn't believe I'd been so wrong about you. And it seemed far worse than Paul's betrayal because the way I felt about him was only a pale imitation of what I thought I'd found with you. Then I told myself how ridiculous I was being. It had only really been one night after all, but it was so hard to put it into perspective.'

Jack nodded. 'I felt the same. I couldn't forget. I thought I'd got past it but then I saw you again and it all came back as though it was yesterday. And then I learned you had a daughter and I assumed you had found someone else and got married and I knew there was no point remembering any more.'

'Assumptions,' Hannah murmured. 'Dangerous things.'

'I wasn't completely wrong, though, was I? There had been someone else.'

'There was only Olivia's father,' Hannah said carefully, her heart thumping painfully. 'He wasn't around by the time I knew I was pregnant and my trust in men had been shattered too deeply to want to do anything but manage on my own.'

Jack held her gaze and Hannah was engulfed by the understanding and compassion he was projecting. Had he forgiven her, both for that note and for not telling him about Olivia?

'Do you want me to tell you who Olivia's father is?'

Jack still held her gaze. 'No,' he said very softly. 'I don't think you need to tell me that, do you?'

'No.' Hannah dropped her gaze as she breathed out a soft sigh of pure relief.

He *knew*. Maybe he had guessed long ago, which would hardly have been surprising. How could he have looked into a set of brown eyes so identical to his own and not know? Or received one of Olivia's frequent cuddles and not felt the same pull that Hannah did on her heartstrings. Or noticed how often his laughter and that of his daughter melded into a single sound.

'You've managed perfectly,' Jack told her quietly. 'You've created the most wonderful home and raised a very wonderful child.' He smiled. 'I thought it was a bit odd that Ben had made friends with someone so much younger than him, but I can understand why it happened now.'

Hannah nodded. The instinctive recognition of a genetic bond had occurred to her also.

'Anyone would fall for Livvy,' Jack added softly.

Hannah nodded again as she waited for Jack to acknowledge his daughter aloud, but he simply smiled and so Hannah smiled back. Maybe that was all that was needed right now. The unspoken acknowledgement of a connection that went beyond whatever they'd had in the past. A connection that could help take them into a shared future. They were still smiling at each other when the children came back to interrupt them. Hannah was not bothered by the fact that Jack didn't want to discuss any issues to do with Olivia's paternity just yet. There was plenty of time to decide how and when to tell the children. Maybe Jack was waiting to see if there was a real possibility that they could become a family, and Hannah had no argument with that intention.

The prospect gained appeal with every passing day. Hannah revelled in the sheer bliss of being in love again. Time away from Jack only intensified the desire to be with him again and the more time they spent together the closer Hannah wanted them to be. Every conversation and shared glance added to that desire for closeness and it reached its inevitable peak less than a week later.

Jack had been caught by an emergency when he was already running late. It was nearly 11 p.m. by the time he knocked softly on Hannah's back door.

'I'm *so* sorry about this.'

'It's not a problem. Livvy has a spare bed in her room. They're both sound asleep. They have been for hours.'

Jack looked at the tousled hair of his son buried in the pillow and sighed. 'I hate to wake him to take him home,' he said quietly.

'Then don't,' Hannah whispered back.

'You mean come back and get him in the morning?'

'No.' Hannah reached out and took hold of Jack's hand. 'I mean…why don't you stay?'

It was easy to pull him closer. They were used to exchanging kisses now when they met or said goodbye or when they thought the children weren't watching. But this kiss was different. Hannah met the touch of Jack's tongue with an answering caress of her own. She let him guide her away from the door of Olivia's room and press her back against the wall of the hallway. She pushed her fingers into the dark curls of his hair, mirroring the feel of Jack's hands as they cradled her head and tilted her mouth for better access. They surfaced just long enough for Jack to pin her eyes with a gaze so intense it burned.

'Are you sure you want this, Hannah?'

'Oh…yes.' Hannah had to close her eyes against the heat. 'I'm sure.'

It wasn't just her eyes that felt the heat as Jack swooped her into his arms and carried her to the far end of the hallway. He placed her on her feet beside her bed and then kissed her again. Her skin was burning now and Jack's touch was either igniting the flames or cooling the places he touched so the rest of her seemed to burn even hotter. Hannah couldn't tell the difference between fire and ice any more. She was aware of nothing but the need to touch and be touched by Jack. It seemed to take for ever for him to undo the buttons of her shirt and peel away her jeans, but Hannah was unable to help.

She still held Jack's head, guiding his lips back to her own whenever they strayed because of him trying to see what his hands were doing.

Jack was laughing softly by the time he tried to discard his own clothing. 'I need some help, babe.' He took her hands and Hannah found herself unbuckling his belt...unzipping his trousers.

And suddenly five years melted into nothing. It could have been the night before that she had last seen and smelt and tasted Jack Douglas, and none of the excitement or incredible satisfaction had faded. If anything, knowing they could be there to be rediscovered lent an expectation and trust that they would be found, and neither Jack nor Hannah were remotely disappointed.

Instinctively, they kept their voices and laughter to whispers. They kept the room dark and the door closed and neither of them slept even for a minute. Even when they lay in the drugged comfort of fulfilment, entwined in each other's arms. It was not a time for sleep. They had too much lost time to make up for. Too much that had been bottled up and hidden away that needed expression in touch and words and simply in being together as closely as it was possible for two people to be.

'I've missed you, Hannah. I've never wanted anyone else like this.'

'Neither have I.'

'I don't want this to stop. Not this time.'

'It doesn't have to.'

'What shall we tell the kids?'

'I don't think we need to tell them anything. Not yet.' Just like they hadn't needed to tell them about their genetic connection. There were more important things to consolidate first.

'Won't Livvy think it's strange if I'm here at break-fast-time?'

'Not if you've got clothes on. She'll think you've come back to get Ben. Just like he will.'

Jack grinned wickedly. 'I don't want to put my clothes back on just yet.'

'Livvy doesn't wake up till about 6 a.m.'

'What time is it now?'

Hannah had to wriggle away from Jack's arms to find her bedside clock. 'It's nearly five,' she said in dismay.

Jack pulled her back towards him. 'That's good,' he murmured. 'We have a whole hour.'

'What time do you have to be at work?'

'Seven-thirty. Same as you.'

'We're going to be awfully tired.'

'It'll be worth it.' Jack's lips were searching for Hannah's yet again. She could feel his smile. 'Next time I might let you get some sleep,' he whispered.

He broke the kiss a few moments later. 'Then again...' he murmured, 'maybe not.'

CHAPTER EIGHT

DREAMS *could* come true.

Like any good fantasy, Hannah's romance with Jack blossomed as profusely as the old apple and pear trees in her orchard. It was meant to be. Other single parents coming together invariably had tension-provoking issues such as angst from ex-partners or children who were emotionally threatened by a blended family situation. Hannah and Jack faced no such difficulties. Nobody could query the sole custody of their respective offspring and the children themselves had the future mapped out far more thoroughly than their parents were aware of.

Hannah was planting some marigold plants into terracotta pots one afternoon, having brought Ben home with Olivia from the day care centre. As usual now, the children had taken their afternoon tea into the shady interior of the macrocarpa hedge hut. Hannah could hear them clearly from beyond the screen of the dense evergreen exterior.

'Where's your mummy?' Olivia asked curiously.

'I haven't got one.'

'Why not?' Hannah smiled at the words obviously being produced with some effort from a mouthful of chocolate-chip biscuit.

'She's dead. Why haven't you got a dad?'

'I don't need one.' Olivia sounded surprised. 'I've got Mummy.'

'I *like* having a dad.'

There was a thoughtful silence during which Hannah

scooped more potting mix into the base of another pot. She found she was holding her breath as Olivia spoke again.

'I'd like one, too.'

The silence was longer this time. Then Ben said generously, 'I guess you could share mine.'

'OK.' Olivia had taken another bite of her biscuit. 'Do you want to share Mummy?'

'Yeah…I guess.'

'She's the *best* mummy in the whole world.' Olivia sounded offended by Ben's reluctance.

'Well, *I've* got the best dad.'

The silence dragged on this time. Hannah finished firming the last plant into its pot and dusted her hands as she admired the bright orange and yellow blooms. She wondered if the children were going to start arguing about the virtues of their respective parents or whether they might change their minds about the agreement to share. But the issue had clearly been resolved to the satisfaction of both.

'You can have the last bicky if you want, Ben.'

'OK. Cool.'

Hannah hugged the eavesdropped conversation to herself. It was tempting to tell Jack that the children had already laid the foundation for a blended family but she had no intention of putting pressure on either of them to move the relationship forward any faster than it was already going. Ben and Olivia simply accepted the changes in that period of a few weeks which made the transition from a hot romance to a deeply meaningful relationship deceptively smooth. It just seemed to happen naturally.

Ben staying the night once, then twice, then three times in the same week didn't appear to disrupt the children's routine in the slightest. Jack still made it seem as though he arrived at the house first thing in the morning to collect Ben, although now he and Hannah were taking turns to drop the children at day care. Olivia had more people in her happy little orbit to love and she was more than willing to include the extras in any morning welcome or goodnight farewell.

'I love you, Mummy. I love you, Ben. I love you, Jack.'

Hannah's heart would always twist a little when Jack was included. How long would it be before she could call him 'Daddy'? The invitation had to come from Jack, however, and if Hannah was bothered by his preference to ignore the subject she didn't let it show. There was no deadline here after all, and maybe Jack still wanted to be sure of where they were heading before involving the children any more deeply. Hannah was confident it would fall into place as perfectly as everything else seemed to be doing.

Like the boundary change on her property that came through in October. Hannah took Jack on a circuit of the new boundary line one Sunday afternoon, with Ben and Olivia bouncing around them like exuberant puppies. Ben had a long stick he was using to swipe the heads off dandelion clocks. Olivia was gathering any wild flowers she could find and so far had a good selection of onion flowers and sow thistle.

'So the stream is on your property now?' Jack paused to admire the clear water trickling slowly between the healthy bog plants of its borders. 'I'll bet there's frogs living in there.'

Hannah nodded. 'Livvy and I raised some tadpoles last year. It's good to have a place to put them back into once they start hopping.'

'I love frogs.' Olivia shoved her bouquet at Hannah. 'These are for you, Mummy.'

'Thanks, darling.'

'I've got to help Ben,' Olivia explained. 'I need two hands.'

Ben had abandoned his stick in favour of throwing rocks into the stream. 'I'm going to build a dam,' he announced proudly. 'A really big one. I'll stop all the water and make a swimming pool.'

'Hannah might not want a dam in her stream,' Jack suggested mildly.

Ben looked astonished. 'But it's going to be *my* dam.'

'And mine,' Olivia said firmly. 'We'll share.'

Hannah laughed despite the rather poignant reminder of the conversation about sharing parents. 'Let's wait for a really hot day,' she said. 'Then we can build a dam and it won't matter if we get wet.'

Catching Jack's glance, Hannah wondered if he realised just how attached Ben was becoming to the property. Was Jack also starting to consider it his home? She smiled. 'Let's go into the forest. We haven't got any pine cones yet and I've got a really big sack to get filled up.'

The children were off and the race was on to collect cones from the half-acre stand of mature pine trees which was now also part of Hannah's property.

'I'll be able to cut some of them for firewood,' Hannah told Jack. 'But I don't want to lose too many. I rather like having a forest.' She bent to pick up another cone. 'If I plan which ones to cut down, I could make a track.'

Jack held the sack open to receive the cones. 'Sounds like a big project.'

Hannah was looking back through the trees. 'I could

make a track that would lead through the orchard, along the stream, through these trees and then round the bottom paddock and back to the house. It would make a great walk to lead Joseph around.'

'It's a lot to tackle on your own,' Jack pointed out.

Hannah just smiled. Maybe she wouldn't have to do it on her own.

'I could help cutting down those trees.'

Hannah's smile broadened. 'I was hoping you'd say that.'

Jack carried the sack of pine cones back to the woodshed and Hannah helped the children take off their gumboots before sending them inside to wash their hands. Jack was still standing near the shed, staring thoughtfully at the back of her house.

'It's a lovely, solid little house, isn't it?'

'I love it.' Hannah nodded. 'I couldn't imagine living anywhere else.'

'Not too small, then?'

Hannah just smiled again. It would be, if the number of occupants doubled.

'You could add onto it without destroying any of its character,' Jack observed. 'There's any amount of room at the back and it's probably got a good-sized attic with that roof line.' He frowned. 'Hasn't it got dormer windows at the front? Have I just never noticed any stairs inside?'

Hannah laughed. 'There's a manhole in the laundry but you need a ladder to get up to the attic. I've got a few boxes of medical textbooks and things like Olivia's bassinet tucked away there. It's probably overrun with mice up there by now.'

'Not if Sooty and Snow are earning their keep.' Jack's focus had been diverted by the sight of the large cats sunning themselves near the woodshed. 'Why don't you have a dog?' he queried. 'It's about the only pet you're missing.'

'I'd love to have a dog,' Hannah confessed. 'It wouldn't be fair with the hours I work, though. Maybe one day.' She looked down at the wilting bunch of pungent flowers she was still holding. 'I'd better put these in water,' she said. 'Outside,' she added with a grin. 'I'm going to pong of onions for days as it is.'

Jack pulled her into his arms. 'I love onions,' he murmured.

'Mmmm.' Hannah gave herself up to his kiss willingly. I love *you*, she wanted to add. His lips helped prevent the escape of the words and the intimacy of the kiss had the welcome effect of making that silence unimportant.

The need to speak words of love aloud was deepening to the point of pain at times now but still she held back because Jack had not said the words first. Hannah knew it shouldn't matter as much as it did, but she also knew why it mattered so much. She had been the first to utter them with Paul and had been too much in love to worry that he'd only ever echoed her sentiments. The awareness that he'd never told her that he loved her unless she'd said it first had dawned slowly, just as the awareness of his betrayal had.

Jack was not going to betray her. He never had. And Hannah accepted that he needed time to know that his new trust in her was not misplaced. He would tell her how he felt in his own time, just as he would talk about Olivia more when he was ready to. It was obvious that he felt as strongly about her as she did about him. Their love-making, including this kiss, was all the evidence Hannah really needed.

The children may have been unaware of the significance of the time their parents spent together, but many of the staff at Christchurch Central Hospital were perfectly attuned to what was going on. The shared meals in the cafeteria and the extra time Jack seemed to find to visit the wards could have been overlooked, but the atmosphere generated around the couple when they were together was far too charged to go unnoticed.

The impression Hannah got from her colleagues was that of distinct approval. Even William, who used to use lunch-breaks to catch up on discussing patient treatment, started sitting at a different table in the cafeteria. Giving her and Jack a few minutes alone together in the midst of their busy days seemed a contribution everybody was happy to make. The chance for a personal conversation was always welcome and it didn't matter a bit that it usually centred on their children.

'I've got the whole weekend off,' Jack told her on Wednesday afternoon the following week.

'So have I.'

'Let's do something special with the kids.'

'OK.' Hannah smiled her ready agreement. Some new lovers with children would be seeking time away from family responsibilities but it didn't bother Hannah at all that Jack automatically included them in their plans. The four of them were already a unit and that was just how she wanted them to be. She loved the feeling of family it gave them and it made the snatched moments of private conversation and touch all the more special. 'Where shall we go? They loved Akaroa, didn't they? Or we could go to Orana park. Or ice-skating.' Hannah's brow creased thoughtfully. 'There's some fabulous beaches tucked away on the peninsula and lots of bush walks. Do you like tramping?'

'Love it.' Jack nodded. 'And I'd love Ben to see just how big and wild some parts of New Zealand are.'

'We could head for the mountains, then. Or one of the national parks. Make a whole day of it.'

'A whole weekend.' Jack was smiling delightedly. 'A real adventure. Something that Ben will remember for ever.'

Something they would all be able to remember for ever. Hannah nodded happily.

'Where shall we go?'

'I have no idea.' Hannah was laughing at Jack's enthusiasm as she noticed William carrying his tray to the next table. She waved at her junior registrar. 'Let's ask Will. He's into tramping.'

William knew exactly where they should go.

'Head for Arthur's Pass,' he told them. 'And park south of Rough Creek. There's a walking track that takes you through wetlands, up through the forest and right up the spur to the edge of the bush lines. There's a hut on the spur with beds and an open fire you can cook on.'

'Sounds like an adventure a small boy would love.' Jack was listening intently. 'Would it be manageable for young children?'

'They'd love it. There's all the birds to see in the marshlands and there's deer and rabbits and wild goats further up. It's steep country but the track's excellent.'

'How far is it to the hut?'

'Maybe an hour and a half's walk. Bit longer if you need to slow down for little legs, I guess.'

The thought of Olivia's little legs coping with such an adventure was a concern but Jack told her not to worry when they discussed it again later that evening over dinner.

'If her legs aren't up to it, I can carry her. She's only a wee dot.'

'But we'll need packs as well. Sleeping bags and food and things.'

'We'll manage.' Jack sounded confident. 'What's the worst that could happen? I can always make another trip to collect the stuff you'll need to dump when you get tired.'

'I'll have you know I'm very fit.' Hannah couldn't help rising to the bait. 'I've done a fair bit of tramping in my time. I can carry just as much as you can.'

'We'll see about that.'

'We will indeed.'

'So we're going, then?' There was a triumphant gleam in Jack's eyes.

'You bet. As long as the weather's not too awful.'

'Ben will be so excited.'

'So will Livvy. Let's go and tell them, shall we? Livvy's watching Ben play video games.'

The children were more than excited.

'You mean we sleep on a mountain?' Olivia's eyes had never looked so huge. 'In the snow?'

'There won't be much snow left at this time of year, button.' Jack smiled. 'And there's a little house to sleep in. A hut,' he amended, grinning at his son. 'With a dirt floor, like your hut.'

Ben's face was shining. 'And we get to cook on a fire? Like cowboys do?'

'Absolutely. What would you like to cook?'

'Sausages.'

'I *love* sausages,' Olivia said breathlessly.

'Do we sleep on the dirt?'

'There's some beds,' Jack said. 'But you can sleep on the dirt if you really want to.'

'I'm going to sleep in the dirt with Ben,' Olivia declared.

'Where are you going to sleep, Dad?'

'In a bed, I expect.'

'Me, too.' Hannah had been quite content to watch and listen to the discussion so far.

Olivia was climbing onto Jack's knee. 'Are you going to sleep with Mummy?'

Jack caught Hannah's gaze over the head of her daughter with an appeal for help written all over his face, but she just grinned. He could get himself out of that one.

'We're all going to sleep together,' Jack said cautiously. 'In the same little house. Like families do.'

Hannah's grin softened and her gaze locked with Jack's again. It *was* a family thing to do. And maybe it would just be the first of many.

Peter seemed to share Hannah's vision of a future family when he popped into her office the following day.

'I'm so pleased for you, Hannah. You're looking *so* happy.'

'I am happy, Pete. It's wonderful.'

'And it's so neat. Two broken families fitting together.'

Hannah grinned. 'Yeah. Kind of "Brady Bunch", isn't it? Except that we haven't got six kids between us, thank goodness.'

'I guess two's enough these days, especially with career-minded parents. You will keep working, won't you?'

'Why wouldn't I?'

'You might want to add to the bunch after you and Jack get married.'

'We haven't even discussed marriage, Pete.' Hannah shook her head. What would her boss say if he knew Jack hadn't even told her he loved her yet? 'And I'm sure the thought of more children hasn't occurred to either of us. I've been there, done that, thanks. And so has Jack. Besides, it would be too big a gap. Livvy turns five next month and Ben's two years older.'

'So it would be a second family. That works for lots of people. And you're still so young. What are you now, Hannah? Thirty?'

'Thirty-three.' Hannah smiled as she shook her head. 'You're hopeless at remembering ages, Pete.'

'Not my own, sadly.' Peter was looking thoughtful. 'I still want to get you involved in the private practice, you know. If you ever want to move away from a hospital career, the door's open.' He raised his eyebrows mischievously. 'A couple of days a week as a private consultant would fit in perfectly with raising another baby or two.'

'Go away, Pete.' Hannah laughed. 'I'm quite happy the way things are. You're not going to talk me into having more children so I can come and work in your private practice.'

'It was worth a try.' Peter sounded unrepentant. 'Maybe you'll think about it.'

'No, I won't,' Hanna said firmly. 'I've got other people's babies to think about. I've got at least four newborn evaluations waiting upstairs and I'd better go and get on with them.'

Routine paediatric evaluation of newborns was a favourite part of Hannah's job, especially when there was time to relax and enjoy the interaction with healthy babies and their proud, new parents. Emily Milne was the last on the list for today and Hannah watched as her mother, Stephanie, undressed the day-old infant in the warm nursery. Her handling of Emily was gentle but confident.

'Is she your first?'

'Kind of.' Stephanie eased Emily's arms from the stretch suit. 'The first for me and Roger, anyway. I've got a five-year-old, Sam, from a previous marriage.' She pulled the feet of the suit clear and then made comforting noises as the baby complained about the lack of cover.

'How does Sam feel about having a new sister?'

'She's so excited.' Stephanie smiled at Hannah. 'Not half as excited as Roger is, though. I wasn't sure I wanted another baby but I'm so glad he persuaded me. Roger loves Sam like his own but he missed all the baby stuff. This time we get to do it together. Do you want her singlet off as well?'

'Yes. And her nappy.' Hannah couldn't help her thoughts spiralling inwards. Jack had missed all the 'baby stuff' with both Ben and Olivia. What would he be like, handling a newborn? He would probably revel in it, she thought. She could just imagine him changing nappies, making silly noises to elicit smiles or rocking a baby to comfort its cries. Hannah could see him with a tiny bundle in his arms so vividly. A baby. *Their* baby. She shook herself mentally. Bother Peter for planting such a notion. The appeal was undeniable.

'Let's have a good look at you, poppet.' Hannah turned her attention firmly to the naked, wriggling bundle in front of her. The overall impression was that of a healthy, mature neonate of good size and proportions. 'We'll weigh and measure you first.'

Emily was grizzling by the time Hannah jotted down the final measurement. 'Bang on average,' she told

Stephanie. 'She weighs 3.5 kilos, has a length of 50 centimetres and a head circumference of 35 centimetres.'

'She's dropped a hundred grams since her birth.'

'That's normal. She'll pick it up again fast. How's her
feeding?'

'Getting better. She had a problem latching on to begin with but the nurses have helped a lot.'

Hannah completed a check on Emily's head and ears
and eyes. As she touched the baby's mouth the head
jerked to one side and tiny lips curved with unmistakable
intent. Hannah chuckled. 'I think she's hungry. I'd better
not take too long with the rest of this evaluation.'

The wails of a hungry infant should have been enough
to dampen any maternal urges Hannah was experiencing
but strangely they seemed to increase them. She could
remember the satisfaction of stifling those cries by offering a breast. Handling the chubby limbs, checking
tiny fingers and toes brought back more memories of
Olivia's infancy, above all the sheer wonder of producing such a little miracle of her own.

The memories were just a background hum that did
nothing to detract from Hannah's concentration as she
listened to Emily's chest with her stethoscope between
the hiccupping cries and held the baby's wrists and feet
gently to assess peripheral pulses. The final check she
made was for a congenital hip dislocation and the baby
stopped crying as Hannah manipulated her legs. Her
eyes were wide open and she seemed to be watching the
doctor and waiting for her verdict. Hannah smiled and
tickled her tummy.

'I think you're perfect, sweetheart,' she pronounced.
'But, then, we knew that all along, didn't we?'

'Can we go home today?'

'I can't see any reason why not.' Hannah finished her

notes as Stephanie dressed her baby again. 'You'll have follow-up visits with your midwife booked?'

'Yes.'

'And you're not having any problems yourself?'

'Nothing that sitting on a rubber ring for a few more days won't cure,' Stephanie said ruefully. 'But I can't wait to get home. I hate being away from Roger and Sam. We're going to be a real family now.'

Hannah just smiled. She and Jack didn't need to have another baby to make them a real family. They just needed to be together—the four of them. Just like they would be tomorrow when they set out for their camping trip. If it went as well as Hannah anticipated then it would be the perfect start to spending even more time together.

Living together even. On a permanent basis.

They were almost all packed by 8 o'clock on Saturday morning. There was a large backpack for each of the adults that contained sleeping bags and clothing, food and utensils. Ben was going to use his school bag to carry the picnic lunch Hannah was preparing. Olivia came into the kitchen with a tiny, bright pink bag, the flap of which was the head of a hippopotamus.

'I found *my* backpack, Mummy.'

'That's great, darling.'

'Put in *on*.' Olivia demanded.

'In a minute, hon. I need to finish making these sandwiches.'

'I'll put it on for you, Livvy.' Jack was sitting at the other end of the table, a cup of coffee in front of him.

'Don't let me forget those muffins,' Hannah said. 'They're in the pantry.'

'And don't let me forget that bottle of bubbly that's

in the fridge.' Jack fitted white plastic straps over Olivia's shoulders as she thrust her arms eagerly into the loops. 'At least we won't need to remember a cork-screw.'

'Oh…plastic cups. They're in the top cupboard over the cutlery drawer.'

Jack stood up to find the cups. Olivia twirled round in a circle with her arms outstretched.

'I've got a *back*pack,' she sang.

'It's not as big as mine,' Ben informed her.

'That's 'cos *I'm* not as big as *you*!'

'I'm gonna carry the lunch.'

Olivia stopped twirling. 'What can *I* carry, Mummy?'

'How 'bout you carry the cups?' Jack squeezed the stack of four plastic cups into the hippopotamus bag. 'It *is* a bit on the small side,' he observed.

'I'll get a big bag one day,' Olivia said reassuringly. 'Just like Ben's.'

'You will,' Hannah agreed. 'When you start school.'

'I'm going to Ben's school, aren't I?'

'You sure are, and it's not long to wait now.' Hannah wrapped the last of the sandwiches in cling film. She'd be making school lunches for Olivia before long. Maybe for Ben as well.

Jack clipped the pink bag closed. 'There you go, Liv. Don't lose them. They're *very* important.' He grinned at Hannah as Olivia resumed her twirling then he opened the refrigerator door and extracted the bottle of cham-pagne. 'When *does* she start school?'

'Next month.' Hannah hadn't forgotten the muffins. She pulled open the pantry door. 'Her birthday's on the sixteenth.'

The silence didn't strike her as odd until she was

wrapping the muffins. She looked up to find Jack watching her, his expression curiously deadpan.

'Have I forgotten something?'

'You could say that.'

Hannah frowned. 'What is it? You've got the first-aid kit, haven't you? I saw you put it in your pack.' Hannah had been impressed by its contents. Jack even carried factor VIII in case of an emergency. 'And I've got the maps and my phone and...' She was watching Jack as she spoke. He pushed the bottle into one of the packs and then lifted it.

'I'll put this in the car.'

Something in his tone warned Hannah that whatever she had forgotten was a matter that needed attention. She picked up the second pack and followed him outside.

'What is it, Jack? What have I forgotten?'

'You never told me when Olivia's birthday was.' Jack opened the back hatch of the vehicle and dumped the pack inside.

'You never asked.' Hannah handed him the second pack as she tried to marshal thoughts that were scattering like snooker balls broken by an opening shot. Jack's reluctance to discuss any specifics regarding Olivia's birth had gone on long enough to seem normal. This was unexpected. Disturbing.

'No. *You* never told me.' Jack leaned against the side of the car and folded his arms. 'I never asked who Olivia's father was either.'

'You said I didn't need to tell you. You already knew.'

'No. I said I didn't need to know. Because I thought he hadn't mattered to you.' Jack's eyes narrowed. 'You must have been sleeping with him at the time you made the trip up to Auckland for that job interview.' His huff of expelled air was incredulous. 'There I was, beating myself up for not being open with you about my ex-wife—whom I hadn't been near for *years*—and *you* were just having a weekend off in some relationship you never saw fit to mention!'

'That's not true!' The full horror of the situation was beginning to filter through but Hannah couldn't sort it out any further than the immediate denial that sprang to her lips. 'There was no one after Paul. I hadn't been near a man in more than a year when I met you. I *told* you that.'

'You must have found someone else pretty damn fast afterwards, then.'

'*No*. There's been no one.' Hannah's voice faltered badly. 'Before *or* after you.'

'You told me Olivia had only just turned four.'

Hannah shook her head miserably. 'No. I said she was ''just'' four. As in ''only'' four.' It sounded pathetic. She knew as well as Jack did that she had misled him.

'*Who* is Olivia's father, Hannah?'

'You know who,' she whispered. 'You guessed that night we talked about it.'

'If I guessed then, why the hell do you think I'm asking now?' The words were ground out, each one icy enough to burn like acid.

Hannah was silent.

The air between them crackled with tension. Even the children could feel it as they came tumbling out of the house.

'We're all ready,' Ben shouted. 'We've been to the toilet and everything.' His steps slowed and he stared at his father, his expression becoming uncertain. 'Are we going now?'

Jack's nod was curt. 'Yep. Hop in the car, you two. We'll be heading off in two minutes.'

Hannah's stare mirrored Ben's uncertainty now. 'Are you sure you want to?'

'Are you suggesting we tell the kids they can't go?' Jack jerked his head and Hannah automatically glanced towards the two excited faces peering at them through the window.

'Olivia and I could stay home. Maybe you'd rather just go with Ben. We can talk about this when you get back.'

'As a matter of fact, I think a weekend on the top of a mountain would be a very good place to talk about this.' Jack closed the back hatch of the vehicle with deliberately controlled and quiet precision. He stepped towards Hannah and she could see the anger that darkened his eyes until they were almost black.

'As well as that…' The words contained just the edge of a snarl. 'It will be the perfect opportunity to really get to know my *daughter*.'

CHAPTER NINE

His daughter.

Olivia was *his* daughter.

Jack's fingers clenched the moulded curves of the steering wheel, his eyes flicking yet again towards the rear-view mirror. Olivia's booster seat was directly behind him and the mirror was angled so that he could easily catch a glimpse of the small face with the big brown eyes surrounded by a halo of golden curls. He'd lost count of the number of glimpses he'd stolen in over an hour of driving so far, but the tiny shock wave was still catching just as strongly on each occasion.

Brown eyes. Just like Ben's. Just like his. Why hadn't he noticed that before? Frequently, amidst the excited chatter of the children that was mercifully disguising the relative silence of the two adults in the car, he caught the gleam of small white teeth as Olivia smiled or laughed. He'd fallen under young Olivia Campbell's happy spell some time ago. He'd known he loved the child well before he'd known she was a part of himself, but this was different. Shocking. His world had tilted sharply on its axis with the knowledge that he was Olivia's father and his anger was fuelling an uncontrollable spin.

'The mountain's getting further away, Dad. I can see it moving.'

'It's an optical illusion,' Jack told his son. 'We're really getting much closer.'

'What's an ottical ooshun?' Olivia piped from the back. '*I* can't see it.'

The corner of Jack's mouth tilted involuntarily. 'It's a trick that your eyes can play on your brain. It makes you think you can see something that's not true.' Had his brain been engaged in some reverse illusion in the last few weeks? Making him *not* see something that was so obviously true?

'Can *you* see it, Mummy? The ooshun?'

'I can see the mountains.'

Jack could hear the faint smile in her voice as she spoke to her daughter. If he turned his head enough he'd be able to see her face, but he had no intention of taking his eyes off the road for that length of time. He'd made no protest when Hannah had suggested Ben ride in the front seat of the car. The extra distance between them had been welcome. If it hadn't been for the thought of disappointing two very excited small children he would have jumped at Hannah's offer to stay home, but the initial shock had been too numbing to consider what he was forcing them into and it was way too late to change his mind now. He was far too angry to want to, in any case. Hannah deserved whatever pain she was suffering right now.

'Look, Livvy.' Hannah's determined effort to sound cheerful was transparent. 'There's still lots of snow on the top of the mountains. They look like big ice-cream cones, don't they?'

'Is it *real* ice-cream, Mummy?'

'It's snow,' Ben said knowledgably. 'But it *tastes* like ice cream.'

'Can I have some?' Olivia pleaded. 'Pleeeease?'

'We'll have to wait and see if there's any snow where we're going,' Hannah told her.

'There will be,' Ben said confidently. 'We're going right to the top.'

'Not quite,' Jack warned. 'We're just going as far as the hut.'

'It's a long way, isn't it?' Olivia said.

'Long enough.' Hannah's tone suggested that any distance would be too long right now, but Jack refused to summon any sympathy. He was the injured party here. Big time. He consciously eased the pressure of his foot on the accelerator as his anger resurfaced.

She had *known*, dammit. She had known, chapter and verse, about Donna's betrayal and how unforgivable he had considered his ex-wife's behaviour. And she had dealt him precisely the same blow. History had repeated itself, only this time it was far worse because he had never loved Donna the way he loved Hannah.

She had lied to him. Not just once or even a few times. She had lied in a thousand tiny ways every minute of every day because their time together had been nothing more than a string of deceptions. What other nasty little surprises did she have in store for him? Was Hannah just having a fling with him to make sure she hadn't thrown away something of importance over five years ago? It was taking longer, sure, but was she planning to let him know he definitely wasn't worth having…as Donna had done so convincingly after the night Ben had been conceived?

Well, she wouldn't have the chance because this time it was Jack who'd be doing the dumping. There was no way he could keep hoping they had something going here that would last a lifetime. They'd be lucky if they could make it last long enough not to spoil the children's weekend adventure. Jack glanced sideways at Ben's happy face and gritted his teeth. The prospect of remov-

ing Ben from the Campbells' lives was not a pleasant
one. There'd be repercussions for his son from this that
he'd have to deal with on top of his own issues. He
couldn't begin to quantify what those repercussions
might be, but at least he'd been careful about contracep-
tion in the last few weeks. Hannah probably wouldn't
have taken the initiative over that any more than she had
done that night in Auckland.

Jack couldn't help stealing another glance into the
rear-view mirror. If he'd been careful that night then
Olivia wouldn't exist. Another wry smile tugged at his
lips. The world would be a sadder place without the
existence of his daughter. *His* daughter. She was someone to be proud of, wasn't she? And he would be once
he came to grips with the shock and dealt with the anger
he had for Olivia's mother. An anger that was almost
uncontrollable because Jack knew that the last thing he
wanted to do was to end their relationship. He *loved*
Hannah, for heaven's sake, but he had no choice. There
was no way he could come to terms with this deception.
Not when it was a replay of what he'd been through
with Ben's mother.

Maybe it would have been better to have called this
trip off. The silence as the car journey finished was
strained. Hannah's pale face as she zipped up Olivia's
jacket and pulled a bright blue woollen hat over the
blond curls was pinched and miserable. She didn't look
at Jack as she eased a pack onto her back and she was
already studying the map of the area in its glass display
case in the parking area as Jack locked up the car and
donned the other pack. This was going to be hell. Two
days…and a night, in the company of someone as un-
happy as he currently was.

Fifteen minutes later Jack decided that perhaps it

wasn't going to be so bad after all. It was easy to keep a few paces behind Hannah as they walked, which precluded any need for conversation. The children were well in front and far too interested in their surroundings to notice that their parents weren't speaking to one another. It was also easy to speak to the children and both he and Hannah were managing to sound as though they were actually enjoying themselves.

'Here's another long bridge, Mummy. We're still in the swamp.'

'Look at that fat blue bird.' Ben was laughing. 'It's got great big orange feet.'

'It's called a pukeko, Ben,' Hannah told him.

'It has big feet so it doesn't sink into the mud,' Jack added.

'There's baby chicks, too.' Ben's feet were dangerously close to the edge of the boardwalk. 'I can see three of them.'

The path became too steep for any of them to do more than conserve their breath for climbing as they followed the track into the beech forest. They stopped for a rest and a drink at one point, although Olivia's small legs seemed to be coping with the ascent just as well as anybody else's.

'The trees are hairy,' she observed with interest between gulps of orange juice. 'Look, Ben.'

'It's lichen,' Hannah explained. 'Kind of mossy stuff that likes growing on trees and rocks.'

Jack wanted to ask about the local bird life. He recognised the waxeyes with their distinctive white circles around their eyes and the pretty fantails that fluttered and perched briefly so close to them, but what was that tiny bird with almost no tail? And the black and white one that sang so melodiously? He might feel capable of speaking to Hannah directly by the time they returned down this track tomorrow. Right now he couldn't bring himself to initiate any kind of conversation and Hannah clearly felt similarly disinclined. Thank goodness for the children's good humour.

Olivia handed her empty plastic cup to Jack. 'Put it in my backpack, please,' she instructed. 'I have to carry all the cups.'

Ben stuffed the last of his muffin into his mouth. 'I'm still hungry,' he announced.

'You'll have to wait for lunch, buddy,' Jack said. 'It's time we got moving again.'

'We'll have lunch as soon as we get to the hut,' Hannah promised. 'We must be more than halfway there now.'

They set off again and this time the pace was slower as they wound up the steep track because Olivia was tiring. Hannah took her hand to help her over a fallen tree trunk and then kept holding it as they walked. Ben kept a few paces ahead and Jack stayed at the back of the small troop, too lost in his own thoughts to hear much of the sporadic exchange of chatter ahead of him.

Hannah *could* have told him about Olivia well before they'd started this new relationship. She'd had the perfect opportunity that evening when he'd explained about that phone call. When he'd exposed that part of himself that Donna had damaged so painfully. Why hadn't she told him? Jack watched the rhythmic stride of his legs as he tried to remember how that conversation had ended.

He'd asked what she'd written in the letter she'd said she'd sent. She'd been about to tell him when the children had interrupted and Jack had had to eat that half-sausage marinated in green fizzy drink. He hadn't pursued the query and he had assumed that Hannah had never revisited the topic for the same reason. Because the letter had been a longer version of that note. A character assassination that would have ruined the new space they had entered that evening and put an end to the feeling of connection that had led to Jack believing he'd had another chance with Hannah.

What if he was wrong about the contents of that letter? She might have written to apologise or to let him know she was pregnant. She might have felt as rejected as he had when her letter had come back stamped 'Unknown at this address. Return to sender', as his had done. Jack glanced up. He couldn't ask Hannah. Not while she was holding Olivia's hand. And how would he know if she was telling the truth, anyway? She had lied outright the first time they had met again. The 'just' had been an afterthought. A deliberate addition that could only have been intended to deceive.

She'd been so horrified to see him standing outside her office. Startled enough to drop her paperwork all over the floor. She'd made it clear to Peter that their first meeting in Auckland had been of no importance to her and she'd cut him down to size after his query about day care. She'd been furious. Or had she? Was it possible that Hannah had been running scared? Jack hadn't even known of Olivia's existence at that point, but Hannah had been building her own life around her daughter for more than five years. What if he'd been raising Ben as he had been for the same length of time and Ben's mother had suddenly shown up out of the blue? His relationship with his child would have been threatened and his response would almost certainly have been extremely defensive. He would have been ready to chop any opposition off at the knees, just as he had been the day he'd found his son hadn't been at home with his nanny.

Knowing what he knew now, it gave Jack the grim satisfaction of understanding why Hannah had been so appalled to find him standing on her doorstep that night. She must have kicked herself for having inadvertently invited his son right into her home. What a weird co-incidence that Olivia and Ben had formed such a friend-ship. Or was it? They were half-siblings after all. They had a connection that couldn't be broken even if Jack never saw or spoke to Hannah again. And Jack wouldn't want to break that connection because that would mean losing contact with his daughter.

What a mess. Jack was glad of the distraction that the thinning forest provided. They were entering more open country now where the bush gave way to the tussock and scree slopes of much higher ground. The mountains were visible again and a plateau of flat land with the isolated, small iron structure that would be their shelter for the night.

'It's the *hut*, Dad! And look! What's *that*?'

'Looks like a wild goat.' Jack watched the animal bound up a nearby, precipitous rocky slope.

'Cool,' Ben shouted.

'I *love* goats,' Olivia shrieked happily. 'Except for Horace sometimes,' she added more quietly. 'When he's grumpy.'

Jack could feel the glance that came his way from Hannah. It was a reproach for his withdrawal as much as an acknowledgement of his right to feel so hurt. She knew this was her fault. Had she really believed he could have guessed the truth and then not said anything? Even if she had, it was no excuse for making assumptions about something as important as this. Hannah had a major problem when it came to communicating adequately, and it was just as well Jack wasn't planning to waste any more of his life dealing with it.

'Are there any bears around here?' The solemn query came from Ben.

'No. We don't have bears in New Zealand,' Hannah told him. 'You might see some deer and lots of rabbits and possums will come out when it gets dark. We might get one scratching on the roof of the hut tonight.'

'There's one!' Olivia jumped up and down as she pointed excitedly.

Hannah smiled. 'That's a kea, darling. It's a parrot. Possums aren't birds—they're furry animals, sort of like cats.'

'And bears?' Ben asked hopefully.

'They're a lot smaller than bears, which is just as well because they're not any more friendly.' Hannah was watching the olive green-brown kea and his mates marching purposefully towards the pack Jack had deposited near the door of the hut. 'They can be very destructive, too. So can keas.'

As if to prove her point, a kea climbed onto the pack, grasped the side zipper with strong claws and used its fierce-looking beak to rip off the tag. Olivia giggled.

'What the—?' Jack waved his arm at the large bird. 'Go away!'

'They can strip a parked car,' Hannah told him. 'Pull the windscreen wipers off even. And they'll take off with anything shiny. Don't leave your watch lying around.'

Jack actually looked at her when she spoke, the first direct glance she had received since they'd left home more than four hours ago, but he said nothing.

'They won't get our lunch,' Ben declared. He was clutching his schoolbag tightly. 'I'm guarding it.'

They got at least half of Olivia's sandwich, however, when she discovered how tame the wild parrots were.

'Throw it on the ground,' Jack advised. 'You don't want those big beaks anywhere near your little fingers.'

'They won't get my little fingers,' Olivia assured him. She balled her hands into tight fists and showed Jack. 'I'm guarding them, see?'

'Look, Livvy.' Ben had finished eating and wandered over to a rocky patch of ground amongst the tussock. 'There's a butterfly. It's black!'

'Where?' Olivia abandoned her apple and scrambled to her feet.

'There. And there's a… What *is* it, Hannah?'

'A lizard, I expect.' Hannah had only caught the tail end of the scurrying movement. 'Or a gecko. You might be able to catch one.'

'Can I take it home?' Ben's eager question was directed at Jack this time.

'Maybe.' Jack was looking at Hannah again. 'They're not an endangered species or anything, are they?'

'Heavens, no. They're very common. I always used to have a skink or two living in a shoebox somewhere when I was a kid.'

'I *love* stinks,' Olivia declared.

Hannah snorted with laughter and heard a similar sound erupt from Jack. The tension between them seemed to ease just a little.

'We'll go looking later,' she promised. 'There'll be lots more of them further up the mountain on the stony ground. They'll stay out while it's sunny.'

'Let's go *now*,' Ben suggested.

'Soon,' Hannah responded. 'I want to sit for a bit and finish my lunch and maybe have a cup of tea. And Livvy needs to rest her legs for a bit.'

Olivia shook her head. 'I'm not tired.'

'Well, *I* am.' Hannah felt quite exhausted, in fact. Emotional stress was just as draining as any physical exertion.

'You could come with us, Dad,' Ben said persuasively.

'I could,' Jack agreed. 'Soon. I'm going to make a cup of tea first. Want to help me make the fire so I can boil the billy?'

'OK.'

'See if you can find some little sticks,' Jack told Ben. 'Livvy can help you.'

Jack disappeared into the iron hut and Ben and Olivia raced around, collecting twigs. Hannah settled back against a large sun-warmed rock and closed her eyes for a minute or two. Her exhaustion was catching up with her. She had spent the last few hours going over and over things in her head. Especially that conversation with Jack when he'd said he hadn't needed her to tell him who Olivia's father was. It was perfectly feasible that he'd meant it just didn't matter. *Why* had she assumed he'd guessed the truth? Because it had been the easy way out? Or was she just in the habit of making assumptions and convincing herself she was right?

Hannah opened her eyes as the warmth of sunshine on her face relaxed her deep frown lines. It was so quiet now. The children must be inside, helping Jack boil water for the tea. She gazed around her at the magnificent scenery, from the rocky slopes behind with snowy peaks towering still higher, along the tussock-covered plateau towards the forest they had climbed through and then to the steep valley that plunged back into thick bush in front of her. Wide, open spaces. Freedom. So why did she feel so trapped and helpless?

And thirsty. Wearily, Hannah pushed herself to her feet and walked towards the hut. Jack was taking a very long time to make that cup of tea. She found him crouched in front of the open fire inside the hut, carefully tipping boiling water from the billy can into two of the plastic cups.

'Takes a long time to get a fire going well enough to boil water,' he said apologetically. 'Hope you're not dying of thirst.'

'I'm fine,' Hannah said. 'What are the kids up to?'

'I have no idea. They went outside to find you.'

'What?' Hannah stared at Jack. 'They were helping *you*. You sent them to find sticks.'

'That must be nearly twenty minutes ago.' Jack shook his head impatiently. 'Ben was nagging about hunting for lizards. I told him to go and talk to you about it.'

'Well, he didn't,' Hannah snapped. 'I haven't seen either of them since you came in here.'

Teabags floated unheeded in the cups on the hearth as Jack straightened the full length of his body. He stared down at Hannah. 'What?' he said blankly.

'How could you do that, Jack?' Hannah's misery was quickly harnessed into anger. 'How could you just let them wander off? Have you got *any* idea how dangerous this area could be for unsupervised children?'

'I didn't just *let* them do anything,' Jack retorted coldly. 'I sent them to find *you*. I assumed you'd be watching them.'

The sound Hannah made was both incredulous and furious. And he had the nerve to accuse *her* of making assumptions and having a closed mind! Jack looked just as angry. Then his expression altered dramatically.

'Are you saying the children are missing?'

'I'm saying I haven't seen them. Or heard them in

quite some time. They could be anywhere, and if they're lost it'll be—' Hannah stopped herself abruptly. It'll be your fault, she'd been about to say—but what was the point? Blaming Jack, or even herself, wasn't going to help. It didn't matter a damn who'd assumed what. What mattered was that the children were missing and possibly in danger.

'Oh…God, Jack,' Hannah whispered. 'If they're lost, it'll be…a disaster. What are we going to do?'

Jack stepped towards her. This was far more his fault than anyone else's. He'd made an assumption that the children would go and find Hannah, as he'd instructed, and they hadn't. She could have laid the blame at his feet with justification but she hadn't, despite her fear for the safety of the children. His anger with her began to evaporate as a glimmer of his love for her resurfaced. The gleam was enough to know that they could get through this…together. He was in control again. He held out his hand and Hannah hesitated for only a heartbeat before putting her hand into it.

'We're going to go and look for them,' Jack said calmly. 'We're going to find our children, Hannah. And everything's going to be fine.'

They left the hut hand-in-hand and then paused as they scanned the rugged terrain as far as they could see in every direction. Hannah could feel the chill of the clear mountain air on her face and the warmth of Jack's hand still enclosing hers. She could see the party the keas were having with the remains of their lunch and the activity stood out in sharp contrast to the stillness around them. There was no flash of bright blue that could be Olivia's hat. No sound of excited cries or laughter.

No sign at all of two small children.

Jack's grip on her hand increased as if to impart reassurance and Hannah tried to swallow her rising fear. If something *had* happened to Olivia or Ben, nothing could ever be fine again.

The vast and stunningly beautiful reaches of the terrain no longer proclaimed freedom. They shouted danger.

'The tussocks are quite high enough to hide them if they're lying down,' Jack observed.

'Livvy never lies down unless she's asleep.'

Jack smiled. 'I can believe that. Ben was desperate to hunt for lizards. You said there'd be lots further up the mountain.'

They both looked at the rocky slopes. There were plenty of large outcrops of rock and areas of scrub and tussock that could easily conceal small children. Too many of them, spread over far too large a space. Hannah looked back across the plateau.

'They could have headed back to the forest track. Ben liked that stream we crossed. He said the stepping stones were nearly a dam and he wanted to stop and throw some more rocks in.'

'Did he?' Jack hadn't heard that conversation. He'd been too preoccupied agonising over the misery of having been deceived.

'We have no clue what direction they might have gone in.' Hannah sounded desperate. 'Why don't I go one way and you go another?'

'No.' Jack was adamant. 'We stay together. I'm not losing you as well as the kids.'

Hannah looked up sharply. Had Jack heard what he'd just said? Was the layer of deeper meaning intentional? The anger that had been in his eyes all day had vanished.

Now she could see the shadow of a fear that mirrored her own. Was it just for the children?

'We'll stay together, then,' she agreed softly. 'Let's go, Jack.'

Hannah had to stretch her legs to keep up with Jack's purposeful stride. They headed through the tussocks towards where the plateau ended and the more rugged high country pushed upwards again.

'Ben!' Jack shouted.

'Livvy!' Hannah's volume matched Jack's. 'Where are you?'

The sun was still shining but the shadows were lengthening now and Hannah could see wisps of cloud forming into thick ribbons over the valleys. She tried not to think about how quickly the weather could change on the divide. Or how it could snow even in midsummer at this altitude. It took only a few minutes to reach a choice of uphill tracks. Pockets of snow could be seen around the rocks up to their left.

'The snow,' Hannah said breathlessly. 'Livvy wanted to taste it.'

Jack nodded. 'Because Ben said it tasted like ice cream.'

Their voices both rose again as they called for the children.

'Ben!'

'Livvy!'

They listened as the echo of their calls faded but again they heard only silence. Hannah's gaze raked the landscape ahead and her foot slipped on the scree at the edge of the track they were following. Jack's hand shot out to catch her arm.

'Are you OK?'

'I'm fine.' To her horror, Hannah felt tears welling

suddenly and was unable to stop them overflowing. 'No, I'm not fine,' she choked out. 'I'm scared stiff, Jack.'

'Me, too.' Jack pulled her close for an instant. 'For *both* my children.'

Hannah made a hiccuping sound. 'Ben is Livvy's brother.'

'Half-brother.'

'I know.' Hannah scrubbed at her face. 'It's crazy but that makes it feel as though he's half mine as well. I...I love him, too, Jack.'

Jack's hold on Hannah tightened. For a second his cheek pressed against her hair. 'And Ben loves you. You're an amazing woman, Hannah Campbell, do you know that?'

'I feel stupid right now.' Hannah pulled away to start moving again. 'I could have prevented this. I'm never going to make assumptions about *anything*. Ever again.'

Jack caught up with her in the space of two strides. 'Assumptions are only made because you trust someone. Yourself or someone else.'

'Maybe I'm not trustworthy, then,' Hannah said bitterly.

'I could say the same thing about myself,' Jack said. 'But I don't believe that. And I don't believe it about you either.'

'Neither do I.'

'Good. So start having some faith in yourself, Hannah. This isn't simply your fault. *Or* mine. It's happened and we'll deal with it.'

Hannah kept up with Jack's pace in silence for a few steps. 'I didn't mean I didn't believe it about myself, Jack. I meant that I don't believe that *you're* untrustworthy. I should have trusted you right from the start. I should have trusted my instincts about you instead of what I thought was evidence.'

'You had a pretty good reason not to.' Knowing about Hannah's father as well as her last disastrous relationship had made it understandable that Hannah had reacted as strongly as she had to that phone call from his ex-mother-in-law. If only they'd had more time back then to have been more open with each other. If only the letters sent care of National Children's had been redirected instead of returned. Jack glanced sideways. 'When you wrote me that letter—was it to tell me you were pregnant?'

'Yes.'

'And when I turned up in Christchurch, did you think I might make life difficult for you and Livvy? Try and take her away from you maybe?'

'Yes.'

'Is that why you still didn't tell me, even when I told you all about Ben?'

'No.' Hannah shook her head miserably. 'I didn't tell you then because I knew you'd hate me...as much as you hated Donna for what she did.'

After five minutes of hard climbing they were well up the slope and Hannah paused to lean against one of the large rocks beside the track. She had to catch her breath and they needed to stop and look around again because their view of the surrounding area was steadily improving. She panted for a few breaths and then realised that Jack was still listening.

'I didn't want you to hate me, Jack. Because I realised I was...'

Jack's heart was thumping more rapidly than could be attributed to the climb. Was Hannah about to say what he thought...no, what he *hoped* she might?

'Was what?' he prompted softly.

'Was still in love with you.' The words came out as a whisper. It didn't seem to matter any more if she was the first to voice words of love. 'I thought if we had a little time to get closer then you might understand...and forgive me.'

Jack was staring at her in silence. She loved him. She hadn't been with him to check out any lingering but dying attraction. She really loved him. He could see the truth of that in her eyes. Could hear it in her voice.

'And when I tried to tell you, you said I didn't need to say any more. You're so good at guessing some things I don't say sometimes, Jack. I just assumed you'd guessed the truth about Livvy. That you knew you were her father. I'm sorry I got it so wrong.'

Jack tore his gaze away from Hannah's for just an instant as he tried to catch the words he needed to tell her how *he* felt. How much *he* loved *her*. 'I said I didn't need to know because it didn't matter to me that Livvy's father was someone else. I knew I could love her like my own. Just like I knew how much...' Jack turned slowly back to Hannah. He wanted to see in her eyes the response to the words he was about to speak, but something caught the periphery of his vision. His head jerked sideways and his eyes narrowed sharply. 'What was *that*?'

'What?'

Jack stepped away from Hannah. Past the outcrop of rock and off the track. His foot slipped on the loose stones and he caught a jagged edge of rock to steady himself.

'I saw something,' he said tersely.

'What?' Hannah's heart skipped a beat.

'I'm not sure. It was blue.'

'Livvy's hat?' Hannah peered down the slope. A long stretch of scree ended at another outcrop of rock and then disappeared over a ledge screened by tussocks and more rocks.

'Stay here,' Jack ordered. 'I'll get further round and see if I can get a better look.'

He edged around the rock face. The footing was precarious and loose stones were easily dislodged to go sliding down the slope like mini-avalanches. Jack lost his grip on the rock as his feet both slipped simultaneously. He grabbed the long stems of a tussock clump but his weight was too much to find purchase on the smooth vegetation. The avalanche of stones that carried him down the slope gained momentum with terrifying speed.

'*Jack!*' Hannah's appalled cry was loud but still drowned out by the roar of cascading shingle.

'Jack!' she cried again in anguish as she saw his feet connect jarringly with the outcrop of rocks that ended the rapid slide. 'Are you all right?'

It took a few seconds for the slide of shingle around Jack to subside.

And then an ominous silence settled.

CHAPTER TEN

JACK was hurt.

Hannah had to find out how bad it was. She ran back along the track to where a line of tussock clumps and rocks bordered the side of the scree slope. She could sit down and slide carefully from one anchor point to the next.

'Stay there, Hannah.' Jack's voice sounded strained. 'Don't try and come down. It's too dangerous.'

But Hannah was already on her way. She stayed sitting, planning each controlled slide carefully as she negotiated the slope. She saw Jack pull himself to a sitting position and then his head dropped sharply as though he was in pain.

'Are you all right, Jack?'

There was no response as Hannah slid for another few metres.

'Jack?'

'I'm…fine. I've just…bumped my ankle.'

Hannah could see his face clearly now. Jack looked pale and his face was set in grim lines that suggested his injury was rather more than a 'bump'. Hannah caught her breath and in that split second of silence she heard something else.

'Livvy?' Her worry about Jack's injury had pushed her fear about the missing children into the background. The faint sound of her daughter's voice was startling. 'Livvy!' Hannah shouted. 'Where are you?'

The bright blue hat bobbed out from between the rocks very close to Jack.

'Don't shout, Mummy,' Olivia said. She put her finger to her lips in an exaggerated gesture for silence as she lowered her own voice. 'Ben's *asleep*.'

Hannah and Jack looked at each other. And then they both moved. Hannah slid the last distance to where Olivia was perched. Jack turned onto his knees and crawled forward. They both knew how unlikely it was that Ben would be sleeping. He had to be unconscious, which meant that he was injured.

Badly.

'Didn't you hear us calling you, darling?' Hannah clutched Olivia in a hug that made the small girl wriggle to escape. 'We were so close. Why didn't you answer us?'

'I couldn't *shout*, Mummy. I didn't want to wake Ben up. He said he was very tired.'

'Where is he?' Jack was still on his hands and knees. Hannah could see the angle his right foot was making to his leg and knew that the 'bump' had to be a dislocation or fracture. Maybe both.

Olivia pointed towards the tussock beneath the rock ledge.

'What happened?' Hannah kept a firm hold of Olivia's hand as they climbed over the ledge.

'We saw a lizard and we went for a big slide. Ben went crash on the rock and *I* sat on him when I stopped. He had a sore tummy so we had a rest in the grass.' Olivia pulled on Hannah's hand as they stood up on the flatter patch of ground. 'He throwed up, Mummy, and then he said he was tired.'

Jack tried to put weight on his injured ankle as he negotiated the ledge, but he dropped to his knees again instantly with a stifled groan before sliding himself forward to the still form of the little boy lying amongst the clumps of tussock.

'Ben?' Jack touched his son's cheek. 'Can you hear me, buddy?'

Ben opened his eyes. 'Hi, Dad.'

'What hurts, Ben?'

'Just my tummy.'

'Did you hit your head at all?'

'No.'

Hannah was on the other side of Ben as Jack unzipped his jacket and pulled away the layers of clothing. She could see the large bruise that covered Ben's left side from his ribs to his hip. She could also see the swelling on that side of his abdomen.

'Ow! That hurts, Dad.'

'I know. I'm sorry, mate.' Jack's touch was gentle but thorough.

Hannah had her hand on Ben's wrist. 'He's tachycardic,' she told Jack. 'Heart rate of 120. Pulse is low volume.'

'I'm not surprised.' Jack was watching the rapid rise of Ben's ribs as he breathed. Then he glanced up at Hannah.

'Spleen?' she suggested softly.

'Could be. Something's bleeding fast enough to be a problem.'

Hannah swallowed. A hard fall against rock could cause internal injuries that could be serious for anyone. For someone with a bleeding disorder it was immediately life-threatening. Ben was already showing signs of shock from serious blood loss. He was pale and sweaty. His heart and respiration rates were up and the drowsiness indicated a dropping level of consciousness. He had his eyes closed again now. Hannah's jaw dropped as she realised something else.

'The first-aid kit,' she whispered. The kit with the factor VIII Ben was in desperate need of.

Jack's nod was grim. 'I left it in my pack. At the hut.'

'I'll go back for it.' Hannah scrambled to her feet. 'You stay here, Livvy. I'll be less than ten minutes if I hurry.' She was fishing in the pocket of her jacket for her cellphone as she spoke. 'I'll call for help on my way.'

She scrambled up the slope and started running as soon as she hit the track. It was much easier going downhill but she had to watch her footing. If *she* broke an ankle they would be in deep trouble. She hoped Jack had bandages and splint materials in his kit. He needed medical attention himself as soon as possible. Hannah tried her cellphone twice before she reached the hut and then twice more as she unearthed the first-aid kit from the pack. There was no reception. The screen of her mobile stated the obvious.

'No Service.'

The run back up the hill was hard. Hannah's legs ached and her chest burned with every gasping breath, but she didn't allow herself to slow down. Ben's life was at stake here and every minute counted. It felt like more than half her own life was on the line as well. She didn't want to lose Ben. Or his father.

It took nearly a minute of watching Jack sort the contents of his kit and prepare to insert an IV line in Ben's arm before Hannah had caught enough breath to be able to speak coherently again.

'There's no cellphone reception up here.'

Jack simply gave a curt nod of acknowledgement. He tightened the tourniquet around Ben's forearm and

swabbed an area of skin. 'Sharp scratch, sorry, Ben. You
know the drill, mate.'

Ben's nod was sleepy. Almost uninterested. Olivia sat
silently, close to Ben, her eyes huge with anxiety.

'Has there been any change?'

'Heart rate's up a bit. One-thirty now. Can you re-
constitute the factor VIII in that sterile diluent?'

Hannah reached for the syringe and phials lying beside the first-aid kit. She drew up the fluid and added it
to the lyophilised factor VIII, which had been rapidly
frozen and dehydrated to make the stable preparation. It
would need slow IV administration over five to ten
minutes, but Hannah couldn't afford to be here that long.

'There was good reception at the car park. I'll have
to head downhill until I can find where it kicks in.'

Jack nodded. 'We'll need a helicopter if they've got
one available. This will buy some time, but Ben's already shocked and I've only got a litre of saline with
me.'

'What about your ankle? Can I splint that for you?'

'I'm fine,' Jack said curtly. But he wasn't. Hannah
could see the sheen of perspiration on his forehead. He
had taken his boot and sock off while she had gone back
to the hut and she could see the alarming discoloration
and swelling of his ankle.

'Jack?'

'What?' He was concentrating on the slow injection
of the factor VIII.

'How much more factor VIII have you got in your
kit?'

'One more dose.'

'You're bleeding badly yourself. That ankle's fractured.'

'I'll be fine.' Jack looked up long enough for Hannah

to know there was no way he was going to use the factor VIII on himself. 'It's Ben who needs it.'

'What's wrong with Ben, Mummy?' Olivia's voice wobbled sadly.

'He's hurt something inside his tummy, sweetheart.'

'When's he going to wake up so we can look for lizards again?''

'We'll have to do that next time, Livvy.' Jack turned to smile at the small girl. 'When Ben's better.'

Hannah was on her feet again. 'I'll get help as soon as I can, Jack.' She glanced at Olivia. 'I'll be a lot faster if I leave Livvy here with you.'

'Of course.'

'Where are you going, Mummy?' Her daughter's face crumpled ominously.

'I have to go and make a phone call, darling. We need some help to look after Ben.'

'*No-o.* Stay here with us. I don't want you to go.'

'I have to, hon. I'll be back soon. You stay and help look after Ben.'

'But…' Olivia looked at Jack, then Hannah, then Ben, her loyalties clearly torn.

They weren't half as torn as Hannah's. She didn't want to leave these three people. Any of them. But she had no choice. She turned and scrambled over the ledge and up through the tussock and rocks. Then she started running again, every step taking her further away from where she wanted to be. Increasing the distance between herself and the people she loved.

It was just as well the track through the forest was clearly visible because Hannah was half-blinded by tears as she hurtled along it. She had to shake her head and blink hard every time she raised the phone she was clutching in her hand. At one point a single bar of reception appeared but it vanished as Hannah tried to make a connection to the emergency services. She kept running. It had taken well over an hour to climb from the wetlands up through the forest to the hut, but Hannah made it down almost as far as the edge of the swamp in less than thirty minutes. And, finally, her call was answered.

'They're on the Bealey Spur,' she told the control room. 'Close to the hut on the plateau.'

'Is there room for a helicopter to land?'

'Yes. Please, hurry,' Hannah added unnecessarily. 'Ben's father has a bleeding disorder as well. He's not as badly injured as Ben but he could get worse rapidly.'

She sat for several minutes after finishing her call, overcome with exhaustion and emotion. The tears she'd thought she'd left behind in the forest came back with overwhelming strength. Hannah hadn't cried like this since…since she had returned home from Auckland after walking out on Jack. The thought of the man now caring for his injured son and their daughter whilst in pain and bleeding internally himself was enough to push Hannah to her feet and start climbing yet again. Even physical exhaustion like this couldn't override her need to be with Jack right now.

The gleaming yellow metal of the rescue helicopter was hovering over the plateau as Hannah emerged from the forest. She could see the paramedics unloading a stretcher and gear as she ran closer. And then she was leading them up the track and it took only minutes to reach their destination. Jack lay in a scoop stretcher holding Ben in his arms until they were transferred to flatter terrain and separated for further treatment prior to take-off. IV fluids were pouring into Ben now and his blood pressure was stabilising. Jack's ankle was splinted.

He was given pain relief and IV fluids were started for him as well to counteract his blood loss.

'There's some search and rescue guys on the way up,' one of the paramedics told Hannah. 'They'll help you get your gear down from here.'

'I'm going with Ben,' Olivia told him firmly.

'Sorry, sweetie, there's no room. You'll have to stay with Mummy.' The paramedic crouched low for a moment. 'Don't worry. We'll take good care of Ben and his daddy.'

'He's *my* daddy, too.' Olivia's lower lip was protruding. 'Ben said I could share him.'

The helicopter rotors were turning slowly and the whine of the engine increasing, but Jack had heard Olivia's statement. He looked up at Hannah and she could see the moisture gathering in his dark eyes.

'Come and find us,' he said. 'As soon as you can.'

'We will.' Hannah had to back away, clutching Olivia's hand as Jack's stretcher was rolled towards the helicopter and lifted in beside Ben's. Olivia was crying.

'I want to go with Ben,' she sobbed.

'We'll go in the car,' Hannah told her. 'Look, there's people coming up the track. They'll help us carry the packs. They might carry you, too.'

The helicopter rose off the ground and the light on its tail flashed brightly as it turned and swooped over the side of the valley.

'I want to be with Ben,' Olivia wailed. '*And* Daddy.'

'Me, too,' Hannah said fervently. 'And we will be. Soon.'

'Soon' didn't feel soon at all. It was completely dark by the time Hannah reached Christchurch. Olivia had fallen asleep as soon as they had started driving, and she wasn't about to wake up in a hurry. The streaks her tears had left on a grubby face were still evident as Hannah lifted her carefully from the car seat. She had parked her car in an emergency consultant's bay directly outside the department, having had no qualms about displaying Jack's permit for such a privilege. This was an emergency.

A family emergency. The family that should have been together all along had been forcibly separated this afternoon, and the hours it had taken to reach this destination had been more than enough for Hannah to realise that something had to be done to make sure they were never separated again. They belonged together. All four of them.

She wasn't going to waste any time searching the department. Hannah went straight to the triage desk.

'Jack Douglas,' she said firmly. 'And Ben. Where are they?'

'They're both in Resus 1.' The nurse smiled. 'You must be Hannah and Livvy.'

'How did you know that?'

'Mr Douglas said you'd be coming. He's waiting for you.'

'Are they all right?'

'They're both stable. Ben doesn't need surgery but he will need observation for a few days, and Mr Douglas needs to go to Theatre. They want to fix his fracture externally because of the level of swelling, but he's refused to go anywhere until you got here.'

Ben was lying on the bed in Resus 1, propped up by a mound of pillows. He still looked pale and drowsy but his eyes were open and he smiled, albeit wanly, as Hannah slipped through the curtains, Olivia still asleep in her arms.

'They're here, Dad!'

'Told you it wouldn't be much longer.' Jack was in a wheelchair, his splinted lower leg raised. He wasn't smiling as he caught Hannah's gaze. He held out his arms. 'Livvy must be heavy. Let me take her for a minute.'

'Are you sure? What about your leg?'

'I'm sure.'

Hannah gently transferred her burden. Olivia opened her eyes, smiled and then wrapped her arms around Jack's neck, burrowed her head into his shoulder and went back to sleep.

'She's exhausted.' Hannah smiled. 'She was so upset when you and Ben took off without her in the helicopter. She howled all the way down the track. I don't think the poor guy who was carrying her enjoyed the trip much.' Her smile wobbled. 'I didn't enjoy it much myself.' She leaned over the bed to kiss Ben. 'We missed you, sweetheart,' she said softly. 'It's so good to see you looking a bit better.'

'I don't remember the helicopter,' Ben said sadly.

'That's a shame.' Hannah ruffled his curls and gave him another kiss. 'Maybe we could take you out to visit the helicopter base one day.' She looked down to where Jack was sitting beside her. 'We missed you, too,' she told him.

Jack simply nodded. 'We're a family, aren't we? We have been all along, we just didn't let ourselves put the pieces together.'

'And the pieces got pulled apart this afternoon,' Hannah added. 'I felt as bad as Livvy did when you were both being taken away from us.'

Hannah reached out and Jack caught her hand. And then they both spoke at virtually the same moment.

'I love you,' Jack said.

'I love you,' Hannah said.

Olivia opened her eyes. 'I love you, too, Mummy.' Her head tipped back as she turned a sleepy gaze towards Jack's face. 'Are you going to be my daddy now? Mine *and* Ben's?'

Jack looked away, his eyes searching those of his son. 'How would you feel about that, buddy?'

'It's cool.' Ben glanced cautiously at Hannah. 'Does that mean you'll be my mum?'

'I'd love to be your mum, Ben.' It was curiously difficult to get the words past the constricted feeling in Hannah's throat. They sounded almost hesitant so Hannah smiled to show she meant every one of them. And Ben smiled back.

'What do you know about your real daddy, Livvy?' Jack's cheek was resting on the blond curls topping the bundle in his lap, but his eyes were resting on Hannah's.

'Mummy said he was special,' Olivia told Jack.

'Did she, now?' Jack's gaze softened. He still held Hannah's hand in his and his gaze was like another physical contact. Hannah couldn't look away. 'What else did she say, button?' Jack queried.

'She said she loved him very much but he had to go away and he would be very sad not to see me because I was special, too.'

'You are special,' Jack murmured. 'Just like your mummy.'

Hannah was trying to swallow the lump in her throat when she felt a small hand touch hers as Ben reached out from the bed.

'Am I special, too?'

'You bet.' Hannah gave up trying to stop her tears.

'Why are you sad, Mummy?'

'I'm not sad, darling. I'm very, very happy.'

'Why?'

'Because we're together.' Jack answered for her, which was just as well because Hannah was incapable of saying anything just then. Not that she needed to. Jack had just said it all.

Or had he? Hannah raised her eyebrows in a question. She didn't want to make any incorrect assumptions here.

Jack planted a soft kiss on Olivia's curls. He smiled at his son and then his eyes caressed Hannah with their soft glance.

'We're a family,' he said softly. 'A real family.'

'Does that mean we get to live at Hannah's house? With the hut and the stream and the hens?'

It was Jack's turn to raise his eyebrows. He wasn't going to assume anything either. Hannah grinned.

'Of course,' she said. 'It'll be your house, too, Ben. Yours and mine and Livvy's and Dad's.'

''Cos we're a fambly,' Olivia said. She gave a huge yawn as a nurse poked her head through the curtains.

'Mr Douglas? They're waiting for you in Theatre.' She looked around at the scene in front of her. The man in the wheelchair was holding a very tired little girl with one arm and his other hand was linked to that of the woman standing beside him. She was also holding the hand of the small boy in the bed. The nurse's smile was understanding. 'Don't worry,' she said soothingly. 'We'll have you back to your family in no time.'

Hannah scooped Olivia from Jack's arms. 'I'll stay with Ben,' she told him. 'They can find another bed for Livvy in the ward.'

'You should go home and get some sleep.'

'I'm not going home without you, Jack Douglas. Not this time.'

Hannah watched him disappear through the curtains. She sat on the chair near Ben and settled her daughter onto her lap. Olivia put her thumb into her mouth, closed her eyes and snuggled closer. Ben's eyes were also closed. Hannah was about to close her own eyes and snatch a moment's rest when, to her astonishment, a heavily bandaged leg reappeared through the gap in the curtains. It was followed by the rest of the wheelchair which Jack was propelling.

'I just wanted to check that you'd heard what I said earlier,' he told her. 'When I told you that I love you.'

Hannah nodded happily. 'And did you hear what I said? That *I* love *you*?'

Jack grinned. 'I said it first.'

Hannah returned the grin. What did it matter anyway? That they'd both said the words almost simultaneously seemed like magic to her. That they both meant every word they'd said made it absolutely perfect.

'So you did, Jack,' she murmured. 'I'll just have to make sure I'm first next time, won't I?'

An aggrieved voice floated in through the curtaining. 'Mr Douglas—I've been looking for you. You *said* you were only going to the toilet.'

Hannah laughed as she saw the chair being pulled backwards. 'Hey, Jack,' she called softly.

'What?'

'I love you.'

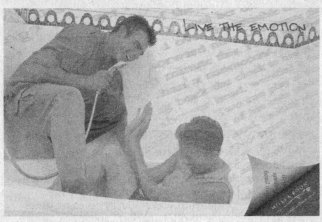

FREE

4 BOOKS AND A SURPRISE GIFT!

We would like to take this opportunity to thank you for reading this Mills & Boon® book by offering you the chance to take FOUR more specially selected titles from the Medical Romance™ series absolutely FREE! We're also making this offer to introduce you to the benefits of the Reader Service™—

> ★ **FREE home delivery**
> ★ **FREE gifts and competitions**
> ★ **FREE monthly Newsletter**
> ★ **Books available before they're in the shops**
> ★ **Exclusive Reader Service offers**

Accepting these FREE books and gift places you under no obligation to buy; you may cancel at any time, even after receiving your free shipment. Simply complete your details below and return the entire page to the address below. You don't even need a stamp!

YES! Please send me 4 free Medical Romance books and a surprise gift. I understand that unless you hear from me, I will receive 6 superb new titles every month for just £2.69 each, postage and packing free. I am under no obligation to purchase any books and may cancel my subscription at any time. The free books and gift will be mine to keep in any case.

M4ZEE

Ms/Mrs/Miss/Mr...Initials ....

BLOCK CAPITALS PLEASE

Surname ....

Address ....

....

....Postcode ....

Send this whole page to:

The Reader Service, FREEPOST CN81, Croydon, CR9 3WZ